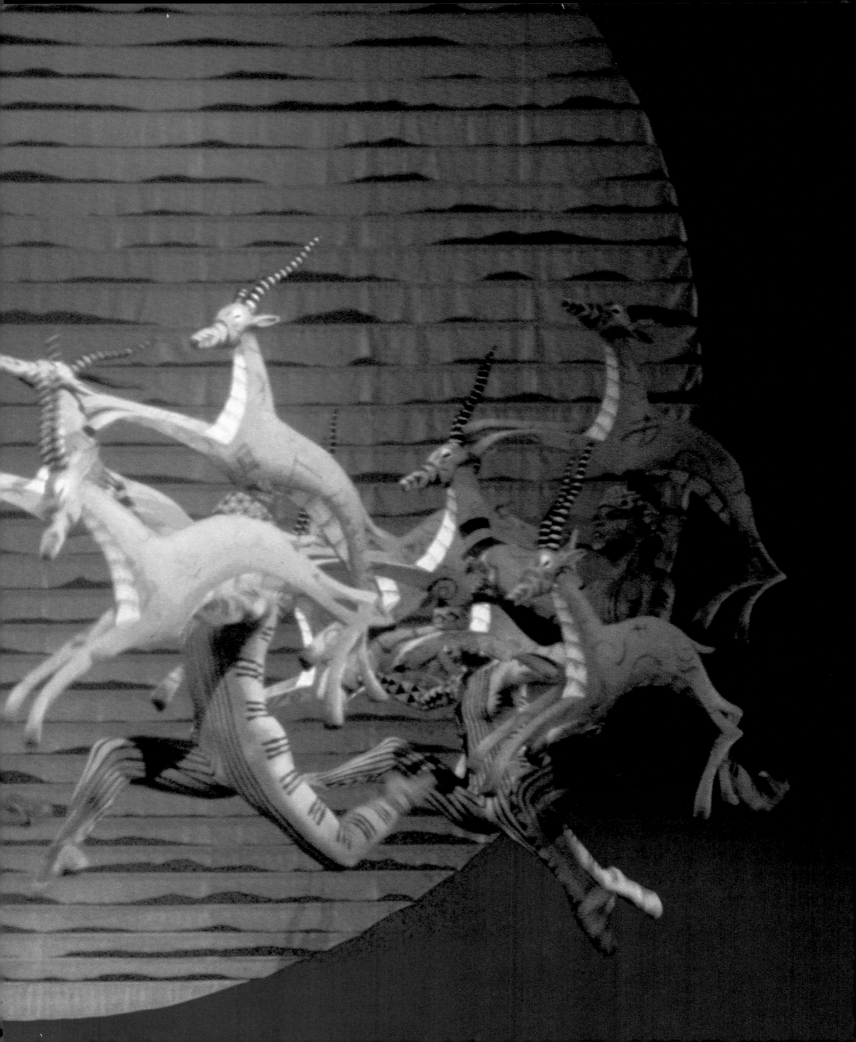

THE LION KING

PRIDE ROCK
ON BROADWAY

JULIE TAYMOR

WITH ALEXIS GREENE

Disney
EDITIONS
NEW YORK

CONTENTS

THE STORY OF HOW OUR FILM *The Lion King* got to Broadway

has many beginnings. I believe I was there for all of them.

The animated feature film *The Lion King* opened on June 15, 1994, at Radio City Music Hall in New York City. Its journey from idea to premiere was fraught with challenges. Several versions of the film had been developed, none of which resemble too closely the movie now playing daily on more than 40 million cassettes on any number of televisions around the world.

In November 1990, Peter Schneider, President of Feature Animation and my partner in all things I've come to call my career at Disney, asked me to produce a film called *King of the Jungle*. I had just completed my first Disney assignment as producer of the animated film *The Rescuers Down Under*. (A small, likable film, *The Rescuers Down Under* did less box office business in its entire domestic run than *The Lion King* did during that fateful opening weekend in 1994).

King of the Jungle was not a musical and bore a striking resemblance to an animated *National Geographic* special. Some of the now familiar characters were there, but the shape, style, tone, design, and sound were yet to be created. During the next four years, literally hundreds of extraordinarily talented people touched the project on its journey from idea to finished film. Most notable among them were the film's directors, Rob Minkoff and Roger Allers; the brilliant Don Hahn, who replaced me as producer when I became the Vice President of Development for Feature Animation and the Executive Producer of the film; the story artists, led by Brenda Chapman-Lima; the screenwriters, Jonathan Roberts, Irene Mecchi, and Linda Woolverton; the supervising animators, including Ruben Aquino, Andreas Deja, Tony Fucile, and Mark Henn; the principle voice cast, led by James Earl Jones, Jeremy Irons, and Nathan Lane; and the extraordinary music and lyrics created by Hans Zimmer, Elton John, and Tim Rice.

The Lion King was interpreted by some as an allegory for our times, a spiritual journey, a broad comedy, a knockoff of *Hamlet,* another story pushing the patriarchal structure, a cash cow, a timeless myth, the next in the line of Disney animated classics. Not surprisingly, no one said it looked like a Broadway show in the making.

Also in 1994, Walt Disney Theatrical Productions came to life under the leadership of Robert McTyre and director Robert Jess Roth, who brought the animated film *Beauty and the Beast* to life on the stage and marked the beginning of a new Disney business.

Like any new venture built on the success of one product, the nascent theatrical division was in search of more options for stage productions. Walt Disney Feature Animation was called on for support. Peter Schneider and I met with Michael Eisner and created a plan that included new non-animated titles as well as staged versions of some of the old animated films. Of greatest interest to Eisner was *The Lion King,* which I promptly told him was the worst idea I had ever heard. He smiled and we moved on.

At our next theatrical development meeting, he asked how my adaptation of *The Lion King* was coming along. I told him again it was the worst idea in the world and that it would be impossible to create a stage version of such inherently non-theatrical material. There was nothing about the film that called out to be theatricalized. Frank Rich in *The New York Times* called *Beauty and the Beast* an animated Broadway musical. No one ever said anything similar about *The Lion King.* He smiled.

This discussion repeated itself several times until Michael grew weary of smiling and told me in no uncertain terms that I was indeed working on an adaptation of *The Lion King.* I blurted back that it was impossible, and he shot back even faster it wasn't impossible, I just needed a brilliant idea!

A brilliant idea, that's it. All I needed to do was *find* someone with a brilliant idea. This sleight of hand is known as *development* in many circles of Hollywood.

Allow me to digress a moment. In 1983, Peter Schneider and I were sharing a nine-by-nine-foot office in the Los Angeles Music Center where he was working on the 1994 Olympic Arts Festival and I was working on a touring theater program for the Mark Taper Forum. The Olympic Arts Festival revolutionized the way Southern Californians viewed the performing arts and gave birth to the biennial Los Angeles Festival. The original mission of the 1987 Los Angeles Festival was to bring the finest and most extraordinary theater, dance, and music to Los Angeles for a four-week bacchanal of the performing arts. Through my association with Peter, I worked as a line producer on the Olympic Arts Festival and ultimately as the associate director of the Los Angeles Festival. At the close of the Olympic Festival, Peter left behind his career in the arts and took his current post at Disney.

The confluence of the festivals, Feature Animation, and *The Lion King* on Broadway began to come together at this point, although no one involved realized it. The year was 1985. Julie Taymor was mounting *Liberty's Taken* at the Castle Hill Festival in Massachusetts. The extraordinary production, originally commissioned four years earlier by the American Place Theater, was staged for only two weeks outdoors in Massachusetts.

The production generated a great deal of buzz, although the buzz at the Castle Hill Festival was mostly that of a massive mosquito invasion.

Meanwhile, back in Los Angeles, I heard about this production and its brilliant designer, director, and conceptualist, Julie Taymor. I reached Julie at home and asked if she would be interested in presenting the piece at the Los Angeles Festival. She said yes, but wanted to know how did I know about it? Had I seen it? Well, no, but I heard about it and would love to see it if it was going to be mounted again. When the photos, ground plans, budgets, and other details of the large-scale production arrived, it became clear that this was not the time for us to work together. I didn't have the resources to present this piece. Now. I knew the name.

During my two years with the festival, I kept hearing about Julie's work. I would tell people that I couldn't make it work for *Liberty's Taken,* and they would tell me about other productions, particularly her work on *The Haggadah* and *The King Stag.* I had missed my big chance to work with Julie and regretted it.

After the 1987 Los Angeles Festival, I rejoined Peter Schneider and went to Disney. A few years later, the Executive Music Producer of the new *Fantasia* project, Peter Gelb, asked if I was familiar with Julie Taymor. He had just worked on a brilliant production of *Oedipus Rex* with her and Seiji Ozawa. I was reminded again of my 1985 mistake.

Finally, in 1995, when Michael Eisner wouldn't let up on my need to come up with a brilliant idea for staging *The Lion King* on Broadway, the answer was, in fact, quite simple—Julie Taymor.

When we met, I could see Julie had a new vision for the project. She was excited by the music, by the setting, and by the opportunites for staging. She was challenged by the task of re-creating something that theatergoers would know by heart, but she wanted them once again to *feel* in their heart. We urged her not to feel bridled by the look of the movie and to create something wholly original from it.

What you will read in this book is how she went about just that. The joy for me has been, and will always be, the process. The journey of *The Lion King* has gone further than any of us ever expected; where it will end only time and new audiences will tell.

Most important to me is that I finally got to work with that extraordinary woman, Julie Taymor.

Thomas Schumacher
September 1997

I WOULD LIKE TO THANK my associate and assistant costume designers, Mary Peterson and Tracy Dorman, as well as my two incomparable assistant directors, Michele Steckler and Dan Fields, for their unbelievable support in bringing *The Lion King* to life. I was blessed with an extraordinary team of collaborators, including Michael Curry, Don Holder, Richard Hudson, Garth Fagan, Lebo M, Mark Mancina, Michael Ward, Joe Church, Tony Meola, Elton John, Tim Rice, Roger Allers, and Irene Mecchi, whose contributions are recounted in the following pages. The exquisite work of the craftspeople and organizers at the 27th Street workshop is greatly appreciated. My thanks to producers Tom Schumacher and Peter Schneider, documentarian Ken Van Sickle, the crew and team of stage managers led by Jeff Lee, and especially the cast members of *The Lion King,* whose inspired performances are the heart and soul of the production.

And Elliot Goldenthal.

Julie Taymor

Antelope performed by Faca Kulu.

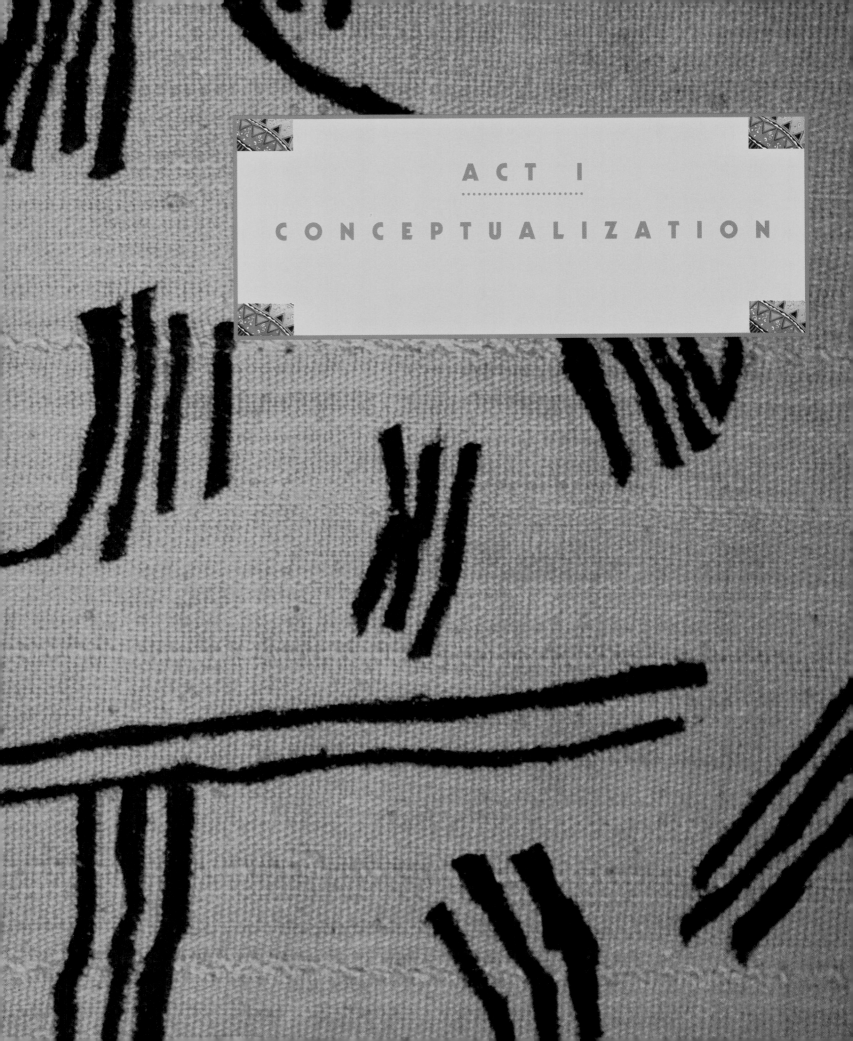

ACT I

CONCEPTUALIZATION

MY ASSOCIATION WITH *The Lion King* began in the form of a phone call from Walt Disney Feature Animation Executive Vice-president Tom Schumacher. A decade earlier, Tom had considered bringing *Liberty's Taken,* a production about the American Revolution I had directed and for which I had designed myriad puppets and masks, to the Los Angeles Festival. *Liberty's Taken* was a picaresque epic that used traditional and innovative puppetry in an enormous theatrical landscape. The bawdy and romantic story took place on battlefields, in brothels, in taverns, in Barbados, on the open sea and had hundreds of characters, both human and animal, performed by an acting company of twenty. Though *Liberty's Taken* was never staged at the Festival, Tom thought my style and design might translate well for Disney's newest theatrical endeavor: a staged production of the wildly successful film *The Lion King.*

At the time there was a great deal of uncertainty about what direction *The Lion King* should take. A spectacular at Radio City Music Hall was under consideration, as was a more traditional stage version. I started to fantasize about environmental, nontraditional settings: taking over Madison Square Garden, or a planetarium or putting up a huge tent and doing the show in the Cirque de Soleil manner. But Michael D. Eisner, the Walt Disney Company's chairman and CEO, was committed to adapting *The Lion King* as a legitimate Broadway musical. So, I set off to devise a concept that would transform the film into a full-fledged musical.

The first step was to develop a script along with a staging and design concept. To maintain the integrity of my own style, while incorporating it into one of the most beloved stories in recent history, was the first challenge to contemplate. The film's imagery is so identifiable and ingrained in the audience's minds. With preconceptions about what the characters should look and sound like, would they accept variations on a theme?

Opposite: Sculpting
the mask of a lioness.

Additionally, many of *The Lion King*'s scenes are seemingly impossible to transfer to the stage: the wildebeest stampede, the panoramic landscapes, the chase scenes, the animal herds, the elephant graveyard, and its hundred hyenas. They are all inherently cinematic scenes. I relished the chance to stage them theatrically. I was not new to working on a large scale and I enjoy transforming the proportions on stage to achieve that play with scale and space. The combination of a dramatic and moving story, the possibility of creating original music, and the enormous size of the project was totally seductive.

THE BOOK

At this initial stage of development I worked not only to expand the story but to determine the placement of songs and choreographic elements, thereby setting the overall concept that would guide the production's visual aesthetic. A musical is a multi-faceted beast, centered on its book, or script. The songs and choreography allow you to cover terrain and show an interior landscape the dialogue can't convey. The inner voices of characters are vividly expressed in song and the power of dance can make nonverbal moments remarkably compelling.

My first focus was the story's through-line of *The Lion King*'s young hero, Simba. The limited 75-minute running time of the film just didn't allow time for Simba to truly take the journey, both inner and outer, that would lead him full circle to his place as king. The two-act stage format provided ample time to deepen and strengthen Simba and show the arduous path that leads to his self-discovery. In every prodigal son story the hero needs to pass certain trials, tests that hurdle him to the bottom before he is allowed to come back on top. Simba, in this coming of age saga, needed to earn his homecoming to Pride Rock. His story needed more detail, depth and conflict. His character, that of a troubled and lost teenager, could use more bite and a rebellious edge.

After working for about a month on my own on various versions of what I like to call "Simba's lost years," I joined forces with the film's co-director, Roger Allers, and screenwriter, Irene Mecchi, to discuss the script, scene by scene, to determine what could work on the stage, what needed to be fleshed out, and what had to go. With my input they would be the co-authors of the new script.

Quite honestly I never expected *The Lion King* to go to the stage. I can remember back when we worked on the movie, we used to kid around and say, "Oh, well, this is one they won't put in the theater."

But ever since I was a child I've loved musical theater and for me to be involved in a musical is a thrill. *The Lion King* is dear to my heart. That was a labor of love. Initially I was apprehensive to see what was going to happen to it, but then I became excited to see the film turn into another creation, to see the characters come alive in a new way. Julie's idea of making the people visible within the puppets is particularly alluring (the thought that characters might prance around in fuzzy costumes was not appealing). And getting more of the African music to the forefront also goes to the heart of the piece. The spirit of the film is transferring from one body into another.

Musicals are tough. They are a hard form to do well. I think modern audiences have lost touch with the conventions of slipping in and out of fantasy that musicals demand. Movies, although they are full of fantasy, have a concrete reality to them; you may be experiencing something that's fantastic, but the movies make it seem absolutely concrete. The stage and the musical format ask the audience to participate in fantasy all the way. They ask you to pretend along with us, like kids do.

For me, that participatory magic is what I find so exciting about theater. And that's why for me it's a great opportunity to be turning *The Lion King* into a theatrical piece.

—*Roger Allers*

Irene Mecchi, co-writer of *The Lion King* screenplay, and Roger Allers, who co-directed *The Lion King* film, adapted the film's script for Broadway.

In agreement that Simba's story was number one priority, we discussed a new scene that I wanted of a young man daring his own mortality. In what was eventually called "Simba's Nightmare," the teenage lion has an "I-don't-care-if-I-live-or-die" sort of attitude. Timon and Pumbaa joke about it, but Simba is restless and eager to find danger. He challenges himself and others because, although he cannot put it into words, he has never gotten over his father's death or the subconscious guilt that he was responsible for it.

The climax of the scene occurs when the physically powerful Simba stands at the edge of the river and dares little Timon to jump across. With virtually no sense of mortality and with the total abandon one sees in James Dean in the drag race scene in the 1955 film *Rebel Without a Cause*, Simba goads this small creature and nearly instigates his friend's death as Timon is swept over a waterfall into a pool of crocodiles. The near catastrophe jolts Simba into a horrific flashback of Mufasa being crushed to death by the wildebeest, and the audience steps inside Simba to see the pain with which he has lived all these years.

Another aspect of the story to reassess was the lack of a strong adult female presence. In the film, Simba's mother, Sarabi; Shenzi, the nasty hyena; and the teenage Nala are the only female characters. In general, mothers in fairytales and heroic myths tend to be absent or weak, ensuring that the hero or heroine must struggle on his or her own. We left Sarabi alone. Shenzi seemed to work just fine as is. We agreed that Nala, who has a feisty personality in the movie, could be shaped into a more dimensional character. In expanding her role in the musical her rebellious spirit gets her in trouble with the villainous Scar. He wants a mate for the sole purpose of having children to carry on his line. Nala is an appealing conquest and when he practically forces himself on her, she defiantly rejects him. As a result, though her dignity is intact, she must flee the Pridelands. In the film Nala leaves home to search for food and everyone expects her to return. In the musical she goes into exile, a departure that evokes deep sadness, loneliness, and permanence. Nala's tale is as compelling as Simba's. Later during the development process, we decided to transform the marvelous shaman baboon, Rafiki, into a female charcter. Tom Shumacher said that while working on the film, they often discussed who they were to believe was singing "The Circle of Life." With the stage production, we now have

Rafiki in the form of a shaman bringing us all together as both a character and a sort of force of nature. This strong, essential female presence elevates the entire theme of the circle of life.

THE SCORE

It is impossible to conceive the script of a musical without thinking about the nature of the music and where the songs will be integrated within the dialogue. The film had five songs by Elton John and Tim Rice: "Circle of Life," "I Just Can't Wait to Be King," "Be Prepared," "Hakuna Matata," and "Can You Feel the Love Tonight." Typically a musical has 12 or 15 musical numbers, which meant that additional songs would have to be composed.

I listened to "Rhythm of the Pridelands," the album inspired by the film's score, featuring songs composed by Hans Zimmer, Mark Mancina and South African performer Lebo M. The melodies are soulful and evocative, as is the way in which the music is arranged and performed. The film's score contains vocals that Lebo M helped create with a South African chorus singing in Zulu.

I think one of the most interesting things about our approach to this musical is that none of the composers are Broadway theater people, and so we are drawing upon our varied past experiences. We are not thinking in terms of, "this is how a musical is done." We are thinking in terms of how we want to do it. There are no boundaries. We draw on all sorts of different areas—film scoring, pop tunes, South African choir work. The music for *The Lion King* is diverse. It is African and it is pop and it is incredibly emotional. It is sweeping, it is majestic, it is comical. The emphasis is on the chorus and the percussion, which includes a rainbow of esoteric-sounding instruments. It isn't about timpanis and gongs as much as it is about marimbas and balophones. The biggest challenge is to put together a band that can play night after night and do anything from "The Circle of Life" to the stampede to "Hakuna Matata." That's quite a range of musical styles.

—*Mark Mancina*

Lebo M composed
the African choral music
for *The Lion King*.

For "Rhythm of the Pridelands," the composers created songs from some of the score music and also wrote new songs, mostly in Zulu and all with a strong South African choral center.

Several melodies on the *Rhythm of the Pridelands* album seemed appropriate for specific characters, based not upon the song's content but upon its mood. I selected the haunting "Lea Halalela," now called "Shadowland," and a song called "Lala," now the introspective "Endless Night," as signature songs for Nala and Simba respectively. Both songs were originally in Zulu and needed new English lyrics to be written. These two ballads offered an opportunity to reveal the inner workings of Nala's and Simba's hearts and minds as well as helping to forward their stories. "He Lives in You," with slight lyric adjustment as it was already written in English, proved to be a perfect song for Mufasa to sing to his son. In fact that song had potential to become one of the major thematic anthems of the musical next to "The Circle of Life." The acapella song on the album, "One by One," sung in Zulu except for the words "One by One," actually has no relationship to anything in the story, yet it seemed to belong to the piece in spirit. I decided to use it as an entr'acte number. The entire chorus, flying colorful bird kites, would be situated in the house, singing, as the audience, "One by One," would return to their seats after intermission.

The African rhythms purposely collide with the pop tunes to create a unique sound, and bring the large chorus to the forefront of the production. While the chorus was unseen and their music was the background in the movie, on the stage the chorus becomes visually and aurally a principal charac-

ter. In addition to the conventional orchestral pit musicians I envisioned a number of African percussionists, kora, and ethnic flute players to inhabit the side boxes of the theater and to periodically weave through the action on stage, making the aural experience a visceral and tactile one.

So we now had songs for most of the principal characters and scenes. As I continued to spot more moments to musicalize I realized that Zazu could use a simple "charm" song near the beginning of the first act and, inspired by the text, suggested to Tim Rice and Elton John that they compose Zazu's "Morning Report." Tim and Elton also were enlisted to compose a comic and nasty trio for the hyenas that could segue into a chase tarantella, and lastly they were asked to create a scene-song that centered on the madness of King Scar in the second act.

Later, during workshop development, Lebo would compose various chants to accompany a lioness hunt or a distant walk in the grasslands. I was keen to keep these songs in Zulu as nothing can replace the poetry and mystery of the sound of the language, and it is totally unimportant to understand the literal meaning of words at various places in the piece.

Unique percussion instruments help define the musical sound for *The Lion King*.

FIRST VISUAL IMAGES

As I began to visualize *The Lion King*, the dominant theme and image to emerge was the circle. "The Circle of Life," the song that opens both the film and the musical, sets the stamp for this symbolism. In addition to being a tale about a boy's personal growth, *The Lion King* dramatizes the ritual of birth, death, and rebirth. In the course of the story, a King dies and is replaced by his son, who at the end gives birth to the next King. The land withers and is reborn. Nature's cycle is evident throughout the work.

For the show's opening, when the animals gather around Pride Rock to watch Rafiki present the royal cub to his future subjects, I first imagined a turntable with inner circles that would rise up from below the stage, like a tiered wedding cake. This swirling disc would seem to emerge out of the ground, the animals would walk on to it, and the mechanism would operate like a carousel with circles rising and falling and going in opposite directions.

In addition to incorporating circles, the design satisfied my desire for an essential, stylized version of Pride Rock. I had decided early on that I would not do a realistic rendition of the Pridelands; audiences would not see Pride Rock lunging out, as they do in the movie. I wanted audiences to be released from their memories of the film right from the start. I wanted them to take a leap of faith and imagination. The mechanics of the Pride Rock design helped drive the overall style of the production. Stage mechanics would be visible.

This is a style I have brought to many of my theatrical productions, since staging *Way of Snow* in Indonesia in 1974. Showing the mechanics, revealing the rods, ropes and wires that make it all happen, is something that the theater can do that film and television cannot. They are literal mediums where the spectator is asked to believe in the reality of the image

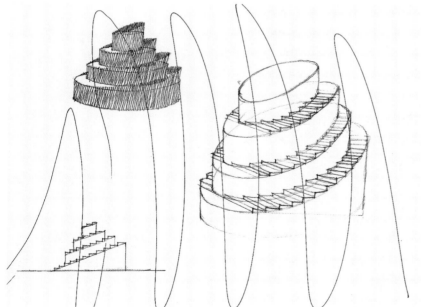

Scenic designer Richard Hudson created this rendering from my initial conception for Pride Rock.

while theater functions best as a poetic medium. The audience, given a hint or suggestion of an idea, is ready to fill in the lines, to take it the rest of the way. They are participants in the entire event.

Magic can exist in blatantly showing how theater is created rather than hiding the "how." The spectacle of a stage transforming, of Pride Rock coming into being before one's eyes, is more visually compelling, more entertaining, than drawing a curtain and seeing the piece of scenery already in place. In a film you cut from one scene to another but in theater the transitions can be seamless and a director's true challenge is the choreography of those alterations of space and time.

Audiences relish the artifice behind theater. When we see a person actually manipulating an inanimate object like a puppet and making it come alive, the duality moves us. Hidden special effects lack humanity, but when the human spirit visibly animates an object, we experience a special, almost life-giving connection. We become engaged by both the method of story telling as well as by the story itself. At every turn I was looking for that which would make this Lion King a live theater event and not a duplication of the film on stage.

In addition to Pride Rock, the other major scenic idea I conceived at this time was to use rolling conveyor belts for the journeys, chases, and stampede that saturate *The Lion King* (I had used a version of this idea in *Fool's Fire*, a film I wrote and directed in 1992). I planned conveyor belts that could be lined up vertically, horizontally, at angles, moving forward and sideways in different formations. During the wildebeest stampede the audience would see actors running and trampling in one direction on top of conveyor belts topped with grass gliding in another direction. The wildebeest would appear to be traveling, albeit traveling in place. Again, there would be no attempt to hide the technology from the audience and scenery would function as a mobile event rather than a static stage picture.

I censored conceptualizing any other set elements, because I wanted whoever would eventually be hired as the scenic designer to be free to propose his or her own creations. Pride Rock and the conveyor belts allowed me to present to the producers, at least at this early stage, a taste of my directorial style and visual concepts.

When you develop any project, whether for movies or theater, it's always a difficult process, because you don't know what you've got. This is the process that happens in all creation, which is that you go around in circles for a long while, until you have that sort of "Eureka" moment, and the whole thing comes together. Development takes time, and the longer you have to gestate, the better.

—*Peter Schneider*

THE ANIMALS

One of the most powerful elements of the film is the rich humanity of the animal characters. Their voices, speech patterns, and emotionally wrought facial expressions are the crux of the humor and the pathos achieved. In considering this ironic duality of the human and the animal it became critical in the design concept not to hide the actor behind a whole mask or inside an animal body suit. I wanted the human being to be an essential part of the stylization. I wasn't sure how to visualize this physical relationship between human being and animal, so I started by sketching various animals that would be a part of the chorus, beginning with the giraffe, a zebra, a herd of gazelles, and a flock of birds.

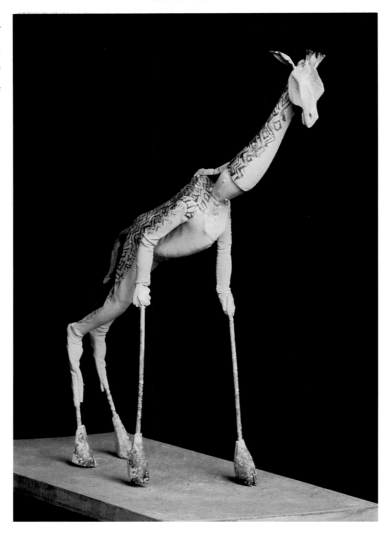

A maquette or miniature model of a giraffe, showing the stilt-like legs that are attached to an actor.

As I experimented with how an actor's body could be incorporated into the long legs and neck of a giraffe, what evolved was a figure created by an actor on four stilts. Nothing is hidden. One is aware that the stilts are attached to the actor's arms and legs and that the giraffe's neck and head rest as a tall hat on the performer's head, so the actor's face is visible. The fact that I could achieve a semblance of the giraffe silhouette was a plus but the fact of seeing the dancer as part of that image became the fun and the point. I wanted the audience to marvel at what a human being can do through true technical prowess. On a practical level, performers sing better without masks covering their faces. Aesthetically and emotionally, an audience gains the facial expressions that can add to an appreciation of what is really a human drama in animal guise.

Opposite: Zebra concepts: The bottom drawing illustrates how the zebra and the dancer intersect so that the human being remains visible. The dancer wears a harness, and the zebra's neck and head extend off the dancer's chest, while the rear part extends off the dancer's back. The performer's legs form the animal's front legs.

For the zebra, my design calls for the creature to be nearly full scale. The zebra intersects the human being, and despite the puppet's height and length, one is still aware of the dancer's body as the zebra cuts through it. The front legs of the dancer are the zebra's front legs while the zebra's head extends from the dancers chest.

The herd of gazelles and the flock of birds involve what I call "corporate puppetry," where one person conveys the essential movement of a group, often by manipulating or wearing a device that carries multiple figures. For instance, five dancers will each bear three gazelle puppets; one on each head and one on each arm, thus creating a herd of fifteen.

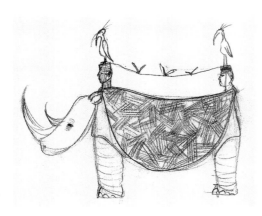

Human beings remain visible within the puppets: Above and right: A pencil sketch of a rhinoceros, and its corresponding maquette. Below: A pencil sketch of an elephant, and a partially completed maquette.

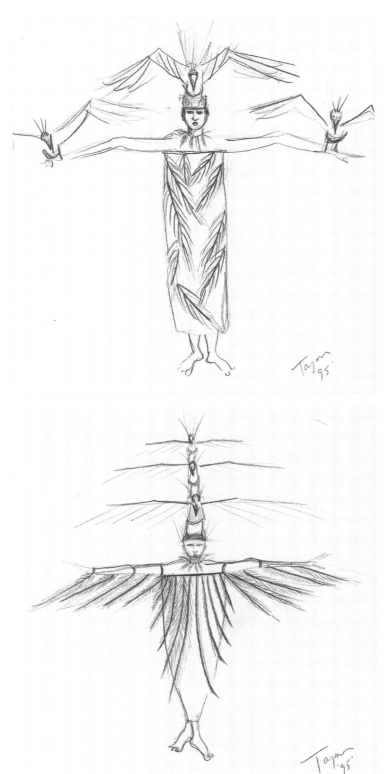

Examples of corporate puppetry.
Two drawings and a maquette explore
ways to convey flocks of birds.

TAYMOR

A color rendering of a cheetah, showing the dancer wearing and guiding the puppet.

Corporate puppetry: a color rendering of gazelles, showing the dancer wearing and guiding the puppet.

Opposite: In a color drawing, the dancer becomes a flock of birds by carrying a totem pole of puppets on his arms and head.
Right: A color drawing of the Ant Hill Lady.

Above and right: A sketch for the Buzzard Pole, and a maquette of the Ant Hill Lady. Motors controlled by each performer cause the buzzard puppets to spin, and the metal spiral encircling the Ant Hill Lady to rotate. More than 100 puppet ants are encrusted on the spiral, and as the spiral moves, the ants appear to climb.

For what I call a theatrical long shot, a device called the gazelle wheel was invented. A dancer pushes a rolling mechanism that rotates wheels with miniature gazelles attached to them. As the wheels turn the animals appear to be leaping, like a carousel. The charm of this gazelle wheel is that the audience sees technology in motion unlike traditional puppet theater, where the wheels would be hidden behind a curtain, in order that the audience only see the leaping gazelles above it. I'm always interested in creating images that have multiple purpose or meaning. In this case the wheels on the device also carry through the dominant symbol of the circle. The audience may not realize it on a conscious level, but circles appear throughout the production design: in the revolving conical spiral that envelops the Ant Hill Lady, in the circular spinning of buzzards on the buzzard pole, in Mufasa's mask.

By first sketching these chorus animals a step toward solving significant challenges was made. Corporate puppetry enabled me to envision transferring the animal herds of the film to the stage. Sketching the giraffe and the zebra helped me understand how to present the animal without losing the human being. And I started to develop a plan for scale play using a wide variety of puppet and mask styles.

Opposite: A miniature model of the Gazelle Wheel, one of the designs which evokes the central image of the Circle of Life. A dancer pushes the rig across the stage and the wheels turn, causing the gazelles to leap and fall as though on a carousel.

PRINCIPAL CHARACTERS

The first person I knew I would hire on the project was Michael Curry. Since collaborating on my film *Fool's Fire*, Michael has been the genius behind the technical design for puppetry in my opera productions of *Oedipus Rex* and *The Magic Flute*. For *The Lion King* we agreed that he would be the co-designer of the puppets and masks. Primarily I would be responsible for the sculpture and

Sculpting the clay form of Scar. In the foreground, sculptures of Simba and Mufasa.

aesthetic design of the characters while Michael would be the architect of the technical design. Obviously the division would be loose; he would have tremendous input into the actual look of the show as I would be very involved in how the characters were going to move.

After introducing Michael to the challenge, we began discussions on the various technical solutions to the principal characters. We talked about the idea of shield masks that the actors could hold in front of them or wear on their arms and backs. For the upcoming presentation to the producers I decided to concentrate just on Mufasa and his villainous brother, Scar. I was uncertain about the degree to which these figures should resemble the ones in the film. I wanted to preserve the flavor of the characters as conceived for the movie, and as written in the script, but I also wanted to maintain my own aesthetic.

An early Mufasa mask showing the orbs that symbolize his heroic character.

I tried to sculpt the essence of each character, to sculpt the expression that would represent the character's dominant trait. In contrast to the continually changing facial expressions in the animated film, a mask can project a single, fixed attitude. The sculptor has only one opportunity to incorporate the anger, humor, and passion of a character, to tell his whole story. It is an ideograph that through movement by the performer or shifting light can seem to change mood. Mufasa is powerful, terrifying, compassionate, all of which I had to build into his face. The essence of Mufasa is symmetry; he is an extremely balanced and straightforward personality. As part of the symmetrical image, I designed Mufasa's mane to form a circle around his head. He is like a Sun God, the center of the universe. He would have orbs around him, rings that represent his mane. There, in the father/hero, the mane symbolizes the circle of life that *The Lion King* celebrates.

I tried to incorporate elements of African sculpture, particularly its plane and architectural severity (a style that is akin to my own). I toyed with the notion that Mufasa's mask should look like it was carved out of wood rather than smooth clay and, using sculpting tools, I created the impression of rough texture. Then, inspired by patterns on African textiles, even by decorative scarring on human bodies, I stamped in and chiseled stylized whiskers, and lines that suggest the beginning of Mufasa's mane.

Scar is a more active force in the drama and has a wider range of emotions than Mufasa. Because he is so misshapen psychologically, I sculpted him with one eyebrow up and one down, completely twisted his face, gave him spiky, porcupine-like hair. In its final form, the Scar mask had a bony, comic yet terrifying feel to it.

I felt delighted and relieved after sculpting these two characters. I saw Disney, I saw Africa, and I had maintained my own aesthetic.

The Mufasa mask was first conceived to operate like a shield that the performer would hold in both hands, rather than wear on his head. The mask lived on a backpack behind the actor, where the rings that represented his mane formed a circle behind the actor's head. The idea was that the performer would reach back, lift the mask up and over his head, then hold it in front of his body, letting it jut forward. This action would be used for the aggressive mode and would allow the character to be more horizontal, lower to the ground, like a lion.

In the first conceptualization, Mufasa's mask was designed to operate like a shield, which the performer held in front of him with both hands. When not in use, the mask lived in a kind of backpack behind the actor. Here, Michael Curry, co-designer of the masks and puppets, demonstrates how an actor would lift the mask out of the backpack and then turn it right side up, in order for the audience to see the mask's face.

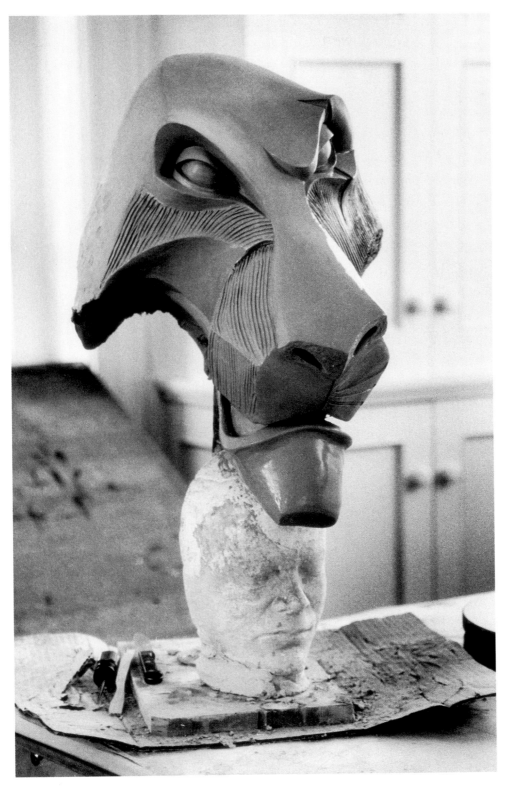

Left and above: clay sculpture
of Scar and Simba.

One of the things about adapting an animated movie into a theatrical piece, versus making a wholly original theater piece, is that there is already a wave of energy to latch on to. Everybody involved in the theatrical conception is capitalizing on something that is already there. The making of the original *Lion King* was one of the most difficult tasks the people involved had faced in their creative lives, because discovering what the film was going to be about and how we would approach the material entailed so much complexity. We would look at ideas and throw them out, and then look at more ideas and throw them out. The Broadway show takes the end result of that and asks how we take this to another place.

—*Thomas Schumacher*

The first Scar mask was intended to demonstrate the two halves of Scar's split personality. I sculpted an enormous mask that Michael then split in two for the actor to hold together on both arms in front of him. When the actor opened Scar's face, holding his arms outstretched, the audience would see the negative on each arm, worn like sleeves. The two halves could face in opposite directions or toward each other in a comic play of madness appropriate for the latter part of the story.

The conceptions of how to wear these masks would eventually change. The Scar mask, for instance, looked spectacular, but when we realized that the actor would be holding his arms out for long periods of time, the design became impractical. But the idea of Scar's split personality generated by this mask would surface later. In the second act, we decided to take Scar to the brink of madness and really play with the notion of his divided personality, play with his dual megalomania and insecurity about being King.

Scar's mask was originally designed to incorporate the two sides of this villain's split personality. Michael Curry demonstrates how an actor would hold the two halves of the mask together, to form the jagged image of Scar's face, and then, wearing the mask on his arms like sleeves, hold the mask apart to enforce the character's duality.

A close—up of one of the
eyes on Scar's mask.

In January 1996, I traveled to Orlando, Florida, to present my ideas to
Michael Eisner. I put forth the changes I envisioned in the script and my desire
to use the music from "Rhythm of the Pridelands." I discussed my concepts for
the scenery and for enabling the audience to see the mechanics of theater. I
showed sketches and maquettes of the giraffe, zebra, the gazelle herd, flocks of
birds, and prototypes of the masks. The concept of the stage mechanics being
visible was the most critical element, and he grasped it enthusiastically. He
understood that a production I directed and designed would neither duplicate
the film nor aim for realism, but would have its own distinctive look and
personality. The production would have enormous scale and aspire toward
elegance but at the same time would not hesitate to reveal the elements that
make theater unique.

The next step was to develop *The Lion King* for Broadway.

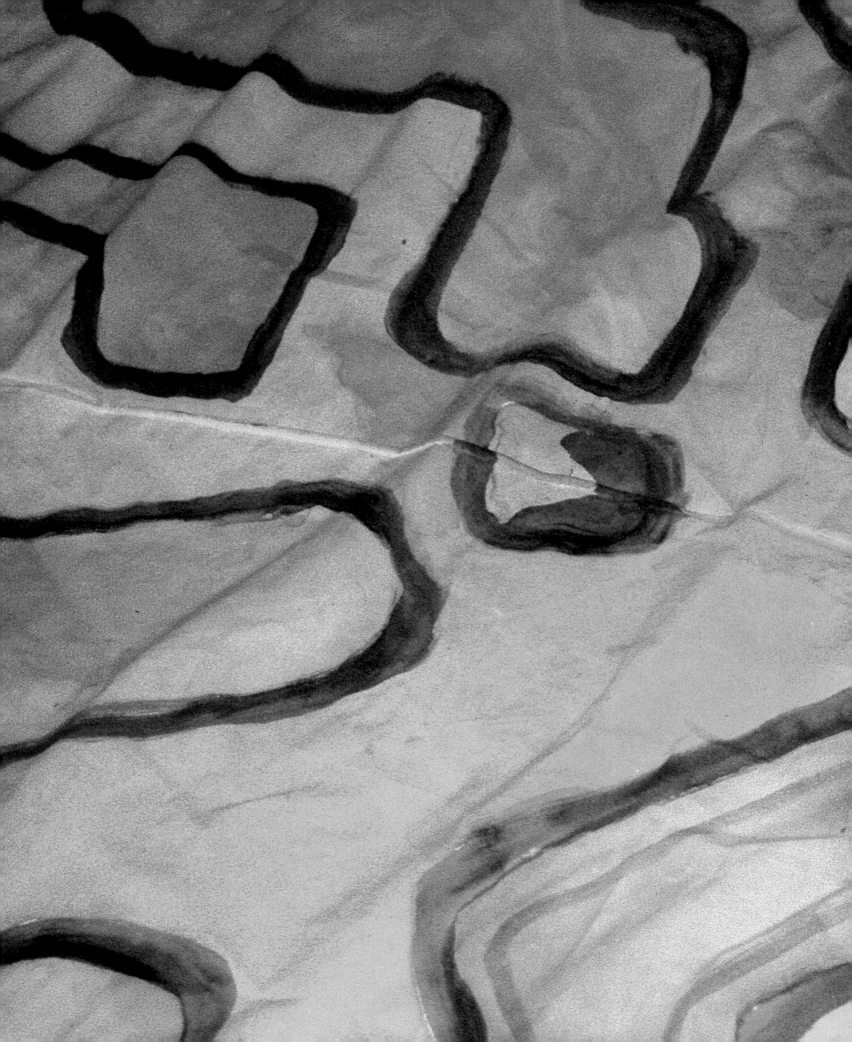

ACT II
....
DEVELOPMENT

Collaborating with (left to right) Michael Curry, Mary Peterson, Dan Fields, and Michele Steckler.

IN EARLY 1996, the big push toward an August workshop began. This workshop would consist of a presentation of costume sketches, prototypes of masks and puppets, and models of scenic designs; a sit-down reading of the new script and music; and the staging of a few key scenes. Quite simply, the workshop would serve as a test to see if the musical was Broadway bound.

One of the most stimulating aspects of the development process is the collaboration with the creative team. On the subject of costumes, associate designer Mary Peterson and assistant designer Tracy Dorman were charged with finishing sketches and overseeing the fitting and building of the more than 250 costumes in the production. British designer Richard Hudson joined the team early in 1996 to develop the scenery, and a short time later, Peter Eastman became associate set designer. Don Holder signed on to design lighting, Tony Meola to take charge of sound, and choreographer Garth Fagan to create the dances. Englishman Michael Ward came on board to design wigs and makeup, and Elton John, Tim Rice, Lebo M, and Mark Mancina were the forces behind the music and lyrics, as they had been for the film. Hans Zimmer's score would be adapted to the stage needs with the contributions of orchestrators Bob Elhai, David Metzger, and Bruce Fowler. Joe Church would become our music director after the August workshop. Helping to keep the world in order was Dan Fields, my new assistant director. Michele Steckler would later come on board as another assistant director nearer to the actual rehearsal process.

Left to right: Composer Elton John with Tim Rice, the musical's inventive lyricist; A. Karl Jurman, the associate conductor, and Joseph Church, the musical director; Michael Ward, the makeup and wig designer, contemplating makeup for Geoff Hoyle, who plays Zazu. Top row: Mary Peterson, associate costume designer, and Tracy Dorman, assistant costume designer; Second row: Richard Hudson, scenic designer, and Don Holder, lighting designer; Third row: Tony Meola, sound designer, and Mark Mancina, music producer; Bottom: Garth Fagan, choreographer.

In an old loft building on 27th Street we found a space big enough to set up a miniature costume shop and a drafting studio for Richard Hudson, and still fit lots of tables where Michael Curry and his staff could construct puppets and masks. It is rare for designers to work in such close proximity; more commonly each artist works in the isolation of his or her studio. Our approach made sense. It is impossible to separate one design element from another. Patterns on costumes were duplicated in the patterns of the scenery. Colors were constantly compared. Everybody had questions about scale, dimension, and the flow of traffic onstage. The loft space gave us easy access to one another and facilitated the collaborative effort.

During this developmental stage, one of my first tasks was to complete the

Contemplating puppets with Michael Curry and one of the craftspeople, Janice Morrow.

designs of the hundreds of animals that populate the story. Having made the decision not to hide performers within animal suits or behind masks, the challenge was to convey the animal's essence while maintaining the presence of the human. I was particularly inspired by the minimalist way animals are portrayed in African art. The style meshed with my visual aesthetic, and reaffirmed that one did not have to represent the whole of an animal's body in literal detail. Sticks or swords could simulate legs; clawlike nails could represent a lion's paw. African-inspired textiles including the graphics of Kuba cloths and fine beading on elaborate corsets provided ways to depict fur, feathers, and skin. The cut of the fabrics, their decorations, tones, and patterns, would evoke an animal's contours and surfaces without sacrificing the character's human qualities.

A spacious loft accommodates tables for building puppets, a small costume shop, and a drafting studio for Richard Hudson.

PRINCIPAL COSTUME, MASK, AND PUPPET DESIGN

Mufasa and Scar were the first lead characters developed during conceptualization; it was time to take them to the next stage. Originally, Mufasa's mask was designed to be stored in a backpack worn by the actor. He could reach behind, lift the mask over his head, and hold it in front of him like a shield. One of the problems was that the mask, when not being held in the forward thrust position, rested upside down on the actor's back, looking rather awkward. The other concern was that when the mask was on the backpack the actor lost the duality of human and animal so critical to the design.

Michael Curry demonstrates how an actor would hold the first Mufasa mask in front of him, like a shield.

With Michael Curry providing technical expertise, we devised a totally new concept utilizing animatronics. The mask was attached to a harness and worn as a headdress above the actor's head. Via a cable control hidden in the sleeve of the costume, the mask could move forward and backward or from side to side. We reconceived both Mufasa's and Scar's original mask along the same lines.

The new masks would preserve the vertical lines of the human actors when worn above their heads, and provide the horizontal shape of the animal when lunging down and

Left: A maquette of Mufasa with the swordlike sticks that operate, at times, like front legs, at other times like weapons.

Below: A maquette of Scar with the gnarled cane that represents a third leg.

forward, suggesting a lion's arching spine and neck. The horizontal form is enhanced in Mufasa by the two swords he is able to use like front legs as he strides regally about the stage. Scar, when in vertical mode, struts about with a gnarled cane, but when he assumes the horizontal animal position, his cane becomes a third leg, implying perhaps that he lost the fourth in the same fight that mangled his face.

A sketch showing a first concept of Scar in Western, formal dress. This was later abandoned for a more African-influenced, abstract angularity of Scar's personality.

A sketch and a rendering of
Mufasa's majestic costume.

To make a mask for *The Lion King*, silicone is brushed or poured onto the front and back halves of a clay or paper mold. This builds up a thick rubber shell, which is held in place by what is called the mother mold. When the mother mold is released from the silicone, there is a lightweight, rubbery skin underneath, and that is the imprint for the mask. The mask is finally made out of carbon graphite, which is a strong, lightweight material. Scar's mask, in its final version, weighs 7 ounces, Mufasa's weighs 11 ounces, and Sarabi's weighs 4½ ounces.

—*Michael Curry,*
Co-Designer
Masks and Puppets

Gooey silicone drips down the front of a clay sculpt that is on its way to becoming a mask. 750 pounds of silicone rubber were used to create the masks.

For the rest of the lioness pride, including Sarabi, similar but more simple masks were designed to sit on the actors' heads like large urns. As children, Simba and Nala do not wear masks but use stylized makeup instead, to suggest lion cubs. Costume elements are added as the characters mature. The teenage Simba and Nala wear stationary masks on top of their heads. In contrast to Mufasa and Scar, Simba has no lower jaw, much like a Roman helmet, giving him a more youthful appearance. I felt it important that his and Nala's masks be smaller in order to feature the actors' faces. The beaded corsets worn by the lions and lionesses are designed to evoke the animals' white belly and, in some cases, to fill in the space between shoulders and mask.

Assistants clean and refine the sculptures that will become the many lioness masks, designed to rest on the performers' heads like urns.

Above: Gina Breedlove
in full costume as Sarabi.

Left: A rendering for
Sarabi's costume shows the
beaded corset, designed to
evoke a lion's white belly.

When Simba becomes a
teenager, he wears a mask,
but unlike the masks for Mufasa
and Scar, Simba's is designed
without a lower jaw—like a
Roman helmet.

Above: Heather Headley
in full costume as Nala.

The costume and mask
Nala will wear when she
becomes a teenager.

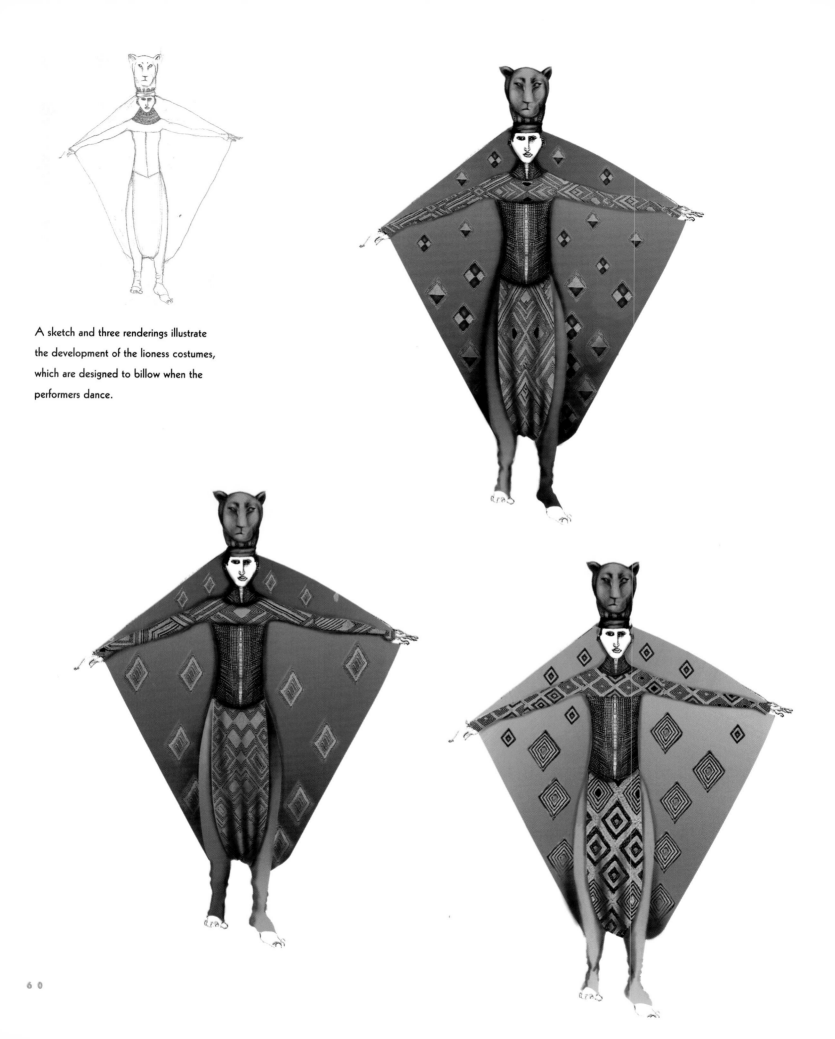

A sketch and three renderings illustrate
the development of the lioness costumes,
which are designed to billow when the
performers dance.

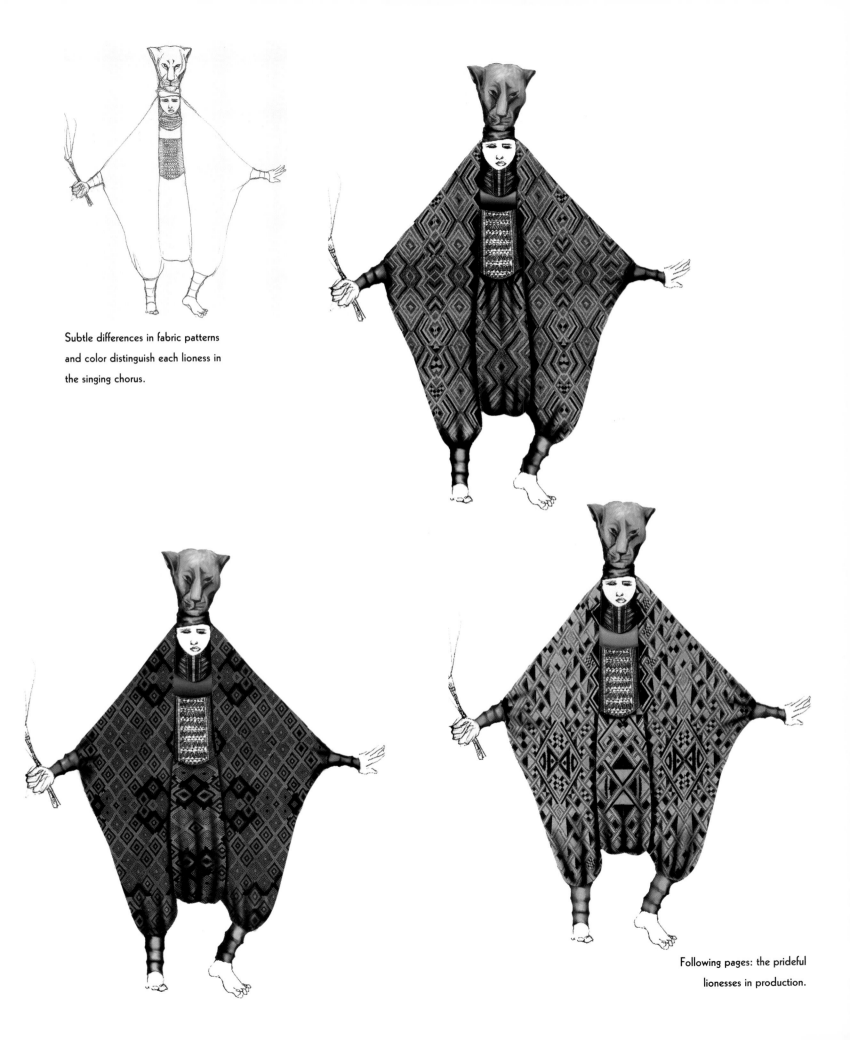

Subtle differences in fabric patterns
and color distinguish each lioness in
the singing chorus.

Following pages: the prideful
lionesses in production.

Wiry, tiny Timon and rotund Pumbaa, the meerkat and the warthog respectively, are the production's comic duo. They are Mutt and Jeff, Abbott and Costello, Laurel and Hardy, all rolled together. Shape and size are intrinsic to the pair's comedy. Achieving this extreme size contrast onstage as delineated by the animated film represented a challenge, especially if dependent on human scale differences.

I decided to go for a puppet solution rather than a minimalist mask approach. To achieve Pumbaa's huge head and belly that live low to the ground, I designed the puppet to be worn on the front and back of the actor. Pumbaa's head is worn on the belly of the actor. Using his arms, the actor is able to open and close the gigantic mouth and at key moments operate a lively, long red tongue. Pumbaa's ears are attached to the actor's shoulders, allowing them to move independently. His hind legs move via lines attached to the front legs of the actor.

The big question was where to put the face of the actor portraying Pumbaa. The solution was to make his head the warthog's hair. Stripes of face makeup lead into a mohawk bristly wig that stretches down the spine. In addition there is a skeletal quality to the exterior of Pumbaa, allowing the audience to see the actor's body between the puppet's ribs and struts.

A maquette of plump, squat Pumbaa, and the actor Tom Robbins kneeling inside the actual puppet.

A costume rendering of the warthog,
bristly wig and all, and the actor
Tom Robbins as Pumbaa.

The sly smile of the Timon puppet.

A rendering of the endearing meerkat Timon
suggests the puppet's diminutive size in
relation to the performer.

Michael and I experimented with different concepts for the Timon puppet. One option was a form of Japanese puppetry in which the performer sits on a squat, wheeled "hachiochi" stool, his feet attached to the puppet's feet. The advantage of this approach is that both the human being and the puppet are the same short height. In the end, we felt the technique was limiting. We then explored using a "humanette," a puppet body that is suspended from beneath the actor's chin, allowing the actor to utilize his own face, perhaps with a little half mask for the

Actor Max Casella concentrates on manipulating the Timon puppet.

character's face. The performer manipulates the puppet's arms, while the puppet's feet are attached to the actor's knees. This can be a very funny vaudeville effect, but unfortunately Timon, rather than looking diminuitive, just seemed to be floating three feet off the ground.

Ultimately, we went for a Bunraku-style puppet. This was inspired by a classical Japanese art form where three puppeteers manipulate a four-foot puppet. After a while, the audience no longer notices the manipulators and just focuses on the puppet character. Our version would have the actor manipulating his own Timon puppet. Needless to say it takes eighty years to become a master Bunraku artist, and in typical Western fashion we were out to demonstrate the technique within a two-week workshop.

Like Pumbaa and Timon, Mufasa's aide-de-camp, Zazu, is an inherently comic character. Envisioning this part British butler, part majordomo, I designed a costume that called for Western formal dress: tails, a cravat, and a bowler hat, in fact. The fabric, an African indigo tie-dye, served to bring the design into the world of the rest of the characters. For the August workshop I designed a version of this costume where the collar of the coat became the wings and tail feathers of the hornbill while the actor wore a large beak as a partial mask on his face. This was an attempt at achieving the small scale of the bird while having the actor's face play a prominent part.

A costume sketch and a rendering for Mufasa's aide-de-camp, Zazu. For the August workshop, the actor wore a partial face mask, and the collar of the coat suggested the bird's wings and tail feathers.

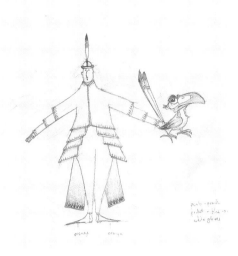

As the costume for Zazu evolves, a suggestion of wings and tail feathers appears in the design of the character's coat.

Right: One of the ferocious but funny hyenas progresses from maquette to mask.

Included in the comedic category are the hyenas, Banzai, Shenzi, and Ed. I wanted a nasty urban feel for this mangy troupe. Torn and patched long underwear with combat boots were costume elements to work in. A hyena has a hump that is higher than its head, providing a natural site for the actor's head. From the hooded hump a spiky-haired bungee cord connects to the mask, which lives on a harness attached to the actor's chest. As the performer dances and moves, he can control the puppet's head via strings attached to his own head. As it is important for these scavengers to be low to the ground, this is one instance where it would be appropriate for an actor to go down on all fours. Crutches extending from the actor's lower arms end in articulated leather hooves. When speaking, the actor slips his hand out of one of the crutches and puts it directly into the mask to move the jaws.

Right: Stanley Wayne Mathis as Banzai in full costume

A color rendering of a hyena.

A sketch and a detailed
color rendering of the shaman
Rafiki, the musical's benign,
spiritual presence.
The costume clearly
illuminates a baboon's
physical characteristics
and proportions.

Last but not least: Rafiki. This shaman baboon stands apart from the rest of the characters as a benign presence who views the action as an outsider while serving as the musical's spiritual center. In the film, Rafiki is male. Disturbed by the lack of a strong adult feminine presence in the story, I realized that this androgynous, comic yet soulful personality could easily be transformed into a female. What's more, she could be the one to sing "The Circle of Life" and the musical's other major anthem, "He Lives in You," bringing a much needed sound to fill out the score. As I was intent on maintaining the absolute humanity of this character, she became the only one who neither wears a mask nor is in puppet form, on or off the body. Vibrant red, yellow, and blue makeup hints at the contours of a baboon's face and allows the actress to reveal the character's whimsical nature through her own varied expressions. The costume humorously plays with a baboon's proportions, accentuating the long arms and short legs by extending the actress's fingers with bamboo tubes and embedding her feet in shoes that are topped with sculpted baboon feet. An elaborate collar of horsehair resembles a baboon's protruding chest, and a low-slung, colorfully beaded butt pad rounds out the comic proportions. Rafiki as shaman is represented by the amulets and magical vessels that dangle from her shirt, the sort of totemic trinkets a medicine woman might well carry with her.

A quizzical Tsidii Le Loka in the exotic makeup that Michael Ward created for Rafiki. The colors and shapes suggest the contours of a baboon's face.

STAGING, SETS, AND LIGHTS

During the development process, Richard Hudson, Donald Holder, and I often worked together in the shop, hashing out ideas and logistics for the staging, scenery, and lighting of *The Lion King*. The script presented several big challenges, particularly in the first act, where major theatrical moments occur one after another. The technical advantages and limitations of The Orpheum, the Minneapolis theater where *The Lion King* would first open, and of the New Amsterdam, where the musical would play in New York, were examined thoroughly.

The challenge for us was to create a sense of vast panorama, an infinite landscape under a wide open sky. Not an easy task on a proscenium stage, which is in essence a box with borders that truncate an audience's sight lines. In searching for the endless horizon, I suggested that perhaps the side masking, or legs, behind the proscenium arch could somehow be made to look as though they were a continuation of the cyclorama.

Richard and Donald designed light boxes to take the place of the traditional legs on either side of the stage. Specifically, these are hollow, translucent Plexiglas rectangles, 30 feet high by about 7 feet wide, with lighting instruments mounted inside. Like lanterns, they can emit light of the same colors and

The first thing I do when designing a production is to note its basic requirements. Does a scene need a huge space or a small area, and is that space up in the air or downstage? When I map that out—especially in a musical, which has so many scenes—I begin to get the shape of the production. Ideally, the audience will always be looking at a different spatial arrangement; each scene should make the audience feel as though it is in a different place.

One of the most remarkable things about *The Lion King* is that it is not set in any specific time. The story could be taking place today or one hundred years ago. I could not peg my designs to a particular date or period as I usually do, and that made me much freer. The design possibilities were endless, so long as the scenery evoked Africa, and so long as it helped tell the story.

—*Richard Hudson,*
Scenic Designer

Philip McAdoo, a palm tree in shadow and light.

densities as the lights located behind the cyclorama, thereby wrapping the stage in a continuous tone, giving the illusion of an enveloping sky. With the cyclorama and the light boxes as a canvas, Donald Holder would be able to create the many shifting hues of a majestic landscape.

The following is a glimpse at how a few of the key scenes and musical numbers were conceived.

I really can't begin the process of designing the show—actually making a light plot—until the sets have been designed, because a number of technical choices depend on the scenery. I need to know where there will be room to hang lights, what color the scenery is, what the height of the scenery is going to be. But in the meantime, I do consult on the ground plan. In other words, I try to protect "real estate," to make sure that, once the set is designed and built, there is space for lighting instruments.

—*Donald Holder,*
Lighting Designer

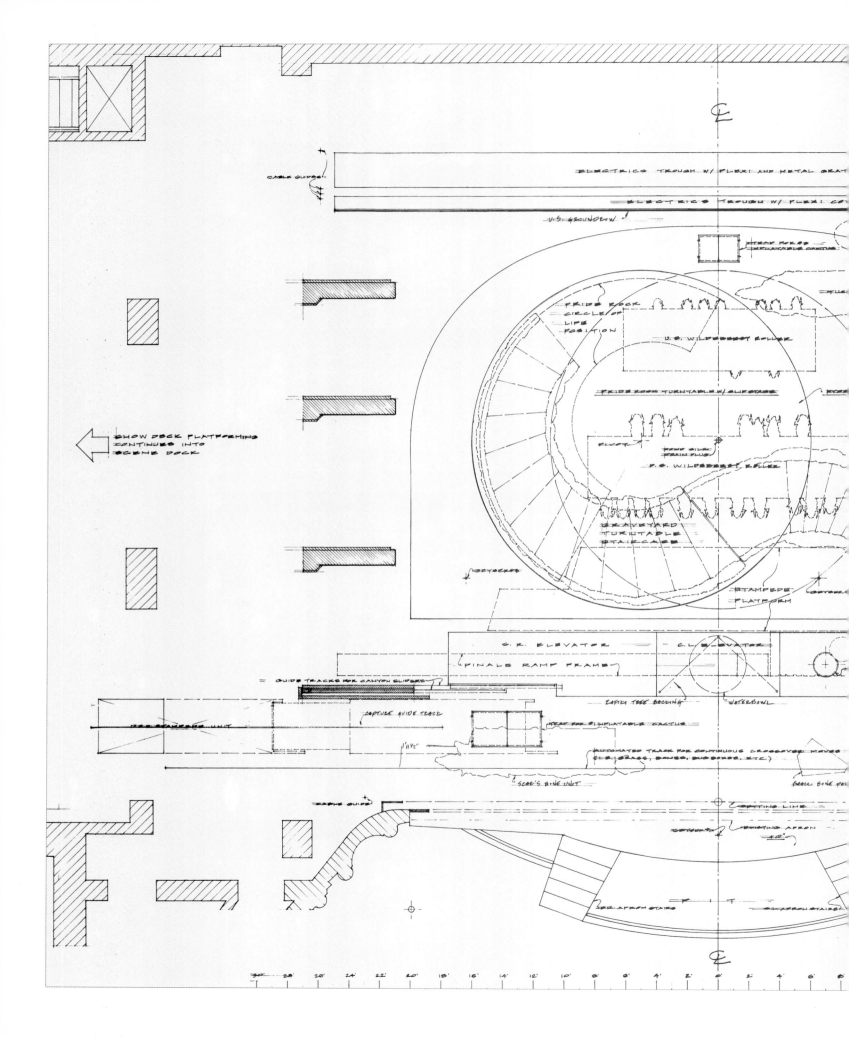

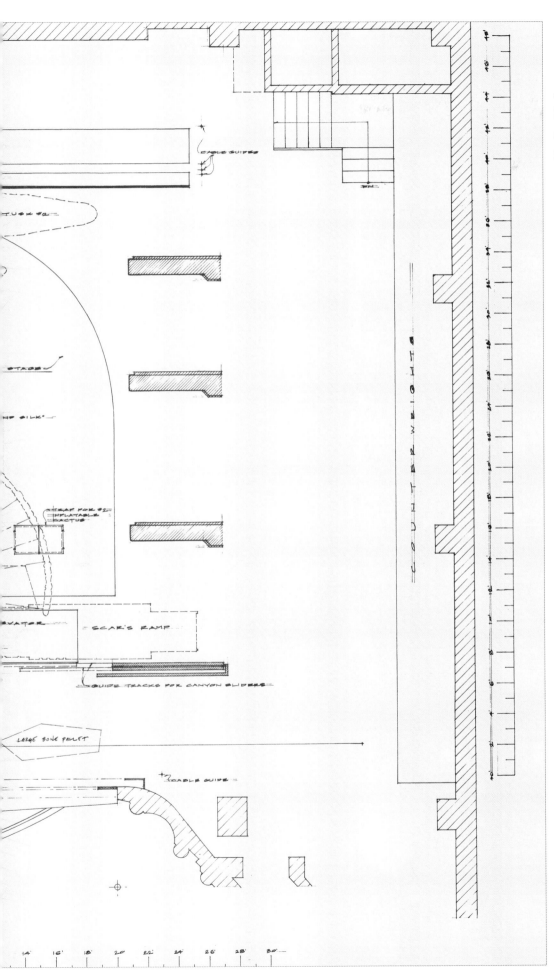

A stage floor plan for *The Lion King*, drawn by associate scenic designer Peter Eastman, shows the central position of the staircase for the elephant graveyard.

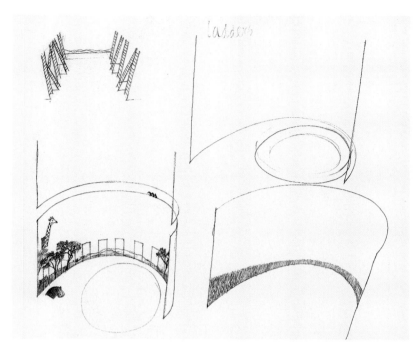

Above: Richard Hudson's preliminary sketches for the opening scene, "The Circle of Life," convey an enveloping cyclorama.

The Circle of Life

The musical opens with the "The Circle of Life." The richly patterned show curtain rises first, followed by the rising of three translucent white borders that evoke clouds and mist. Revealed is an open stage with a patterned floor and ground row of distant mountains, the African savanna where the action of *The Lion King* takes place.

The sun begins to rise. It is a giant, slatted saffron circle made from about 30 ribs of aluminum with silk strips attached to them. It is gently hoisted by wires and gives the impression of the shimmering lines the sun creates on a desert horizon. The silence of this first image is shattered by the earthy chant of Rafiki as she begins to sing "The Circle of Life."

In the film, an anonymous voice is responsible for this song. But onstage, Rafiki, the shaman and diviner, initiates the circle of life, calling animals from far and wide to the presentation of the newborn heir, Simba. Animals move onstage from the wings. The audience hears chanting from beyond the doors of the auditorium, and then birds, cheetahs, wildebeest, and elephants parade down the aisles to join the shaman onstage.

Right and opposite page: Richard Hudson's scenic models for "The Circle of Life" demonstrate the simplicity of his style and the grandness of the musical's landscape.

The proximity of the chorus to the audience immediately reveals the duality of human and animal. Viewers are quickly transported from the two-dimensional world of film to a live, theatrical, wholly visceral experience.

As the procession moves through the auditorium, gazelles leap across the stage, giraffes and zebras gather, Rafiki sings, and from beneath the stage, Pride Rock spirals up out of the ground with Mufasa and Sarabi, the lion king and queen, at the pinnacle.

This page: Richard Hudson's sketches for a revolving staircase, which became Pride Rock.

My fledgling design for the "wedding cake" structure of Pride Rock was quickly rejected by Richard. Too symmetrical. Not dangerous enough. What is powerful about Pride Rock is that it juts forward, forming a jagged promontory. My concept called for one absolutely pure circle within another, and there just was not enough stage power in that image. I heartily agreed with the critique when presented with a much more satisfying, yet still stylized, solution.

Richard showed me the design for a revolving staircase he had created for a production of Verdi's *La Forza del Destino* at the English National Opera. He suggested that Pride Rock emerge from the ground, spiraling upward to a height of 20 feet. The circle symbolism remained intact, but he was able to give the rock an asymmetrical shape that made it more organic to the landscape. Because the structure was part of a huge turntable, we would be able to change the look of Pride Rock by a shift of positioning and lighting, giving us a myriad of possibilities.

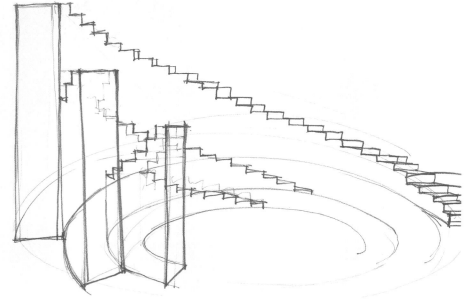

Opposite page: Richard Hudson's scenic model and sketch show the design for Rafiki's tree, which was ultimately made from cloth and sewn onto a drop made of netting.

I was born in Zimbabwe, or Rhodesia as it was then called, and lived there until I was 18. So, in a way, *The Lion King*, with its African sources and context, was a perfect show for me to design. In fact, my first research for the production involved looking at African textiles and their patterns, and at African painting and sculpture. Some of the patterning is used on the stage floor, in the show curtain, and in the symbols and markings embroidered on Rafiki's tree.

—*Richard Hudson,*
Scenic Designer

Originally there was a sort of hemisphere that came up from behind Rafiki's tree. Rafiki was to be sitting in it. She would emerge, and then the hemisphere would revolve so that its concave side faced the audience, and it would revolve again, to display a sort of mini-globe of the world. We made a model, and it looked rather stunning. There was a landscape on it, made out of sand and nails, like those African sculptures that have hundreds of nails hammered into them. It was textured and beautiful and expensive, and it was cut.

—*Richard Hudson,*
Scenic Designer

The Grasslands

In addition to the vast panorama of the Pridelands, one of the strong impressions of the film is the sense of journey, of a moving landscape that can be seen from the perspective of a high-flying hornbill or a grounded lion cub. For the early-morning scene in which Mufasa guides the young Simba through the grasslands to the top of Pride Rock, I designed costumes for the chorus to portray not the wildlife of the savannah but the moving landscape itself.

The audience first sees the tall grass rising out of a long trap that stretches across the stage. Soon they realize that the grass grows out of large trays borne on the heads of 27 performers. As they begin to slowly move about the stage creating hills and valleys, two dancers carrying miniature puppets of Mufasa and Simba move through the grasslands. In essence this is a theatrical long shot, underscored by the chant of the chorus—dialogue unnecessary. As the grasslands form a corridor, the puppets give way to the actors portraying Mufasa and Simba. A close-up. Dialogue ensues as the king leads his son to the top of Pride Rock.

This technique of scale and perspective play has been a part of my theatrical vocabulary and became quite useful in the realization of transitional scenes in *The Lion King*. In addition to the miniature three-dimensional puppets, shadow puppets to be played upon the walls of Scar's cave and in the hollow of Rafiki's tree were designed.

Left: In Richard Hudson's model, the savanna grassland figures line up behind Rafiki's tree.

Far left and below: The chorus of dancers and singers create the African savanna by carrying trays of grass on their heads.

Following page: In production, the grasslands form a majestic background for Rafiki and her mystical tree.

Opposite, and on following pages:
Costume renderings of the tricksters, the
magical henchmen of young Simba's imagination.

I Can't Wait to Be King

The fantasy song/scene in which young Simba and Nala gleefully imagine life without the bossy and protective Zazu was one of the hardest for us to conceive. In the film, it is a short but lavish Busby Berkeley production number, where images happen one second after another.

Having already staged a grand production number for "The Circle of Life," we could not repeat that particular concept. And because the stagehands have to set up for the elephant graveyard, which comes next, there was only a ten-foot strip of downstage space left for a sequence that depicts a child's fantasy and must stimulate the imagination. The scene should be wild and colorful. Except for Zazu, who is costumed in blue, the musical's color scheme runs to earthy browns and golds. Here was one of the few chances to paint with bright colors.

Richard and I considered a couple of approaches, including using scaffolding to form bridges on which invisible puppeteers would stand and manipulate relief puppets in a wall of light. In this scheme there would be a kaleidoscope of mirrors and light boxes on the scaffolding, along with the 27 dancers and singers available to operate the puppets. Because we had such little depth, this solution allowed us to have a vertical playing area behind the proscenium arch, which was to be filled with fantastical floating creatures. Invariably the scaffolding posed an enormous technical problem. There was really no way to store it in the wings, and flying it in from above the stage would have been inordinately expensive. It all just seemed too heavy, noisy, and complicated.

The breakthrough in conceptualizing this number occurred when I stopped being held hostage by the imagery from the film and came up with the idea of the four tricksters. The simple action of the song is the outwitting of Zazu by Simba and Nala. The tricksters are Simba's magical henchmen. Any time Zazu tries to reconnect with Simba, these big, mischievous bouncers are in his way, protecting "King Simba."

The tricksters are distinctly unique in the production. They are fantasy creatures very much inspired by African tribal masks. These are the only characters whose performers' faces are covered. The costumes are quilted and the masks are soft sculpture, so the dancers can tumble in them. They are fanciful

87

TAYMOR

TAYMOR

TAYMOR

TAYMOR

creations of Simba's imagination and look as though a child could have dreamed them.

While Zazu is playfully tormented by the tricksters on the ground, Simba and Nala defy gravity by flying above him on the necks of gigantic floating giraffes. They clamber upon the backs of ostriches, leap from one trickster to another, land on the floor and fly up again, somersaulting into the sky. The use of flight in this scene satisfied not only the young Simba's fantasy but also the practical needs of utilizing a vertical playing space.

Above and opposite: Fanciful giraffes and ostriches populate Simba's rambunctious fantasy of when he will be king.

Following pages: Young Nala (Kajuana Shuford) and Simba (Scott Irby-Ranniar) cavort on stage with their extravagant menagerie.

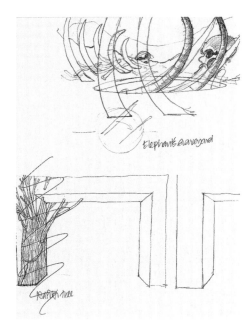

Richard Hudson's sketches and models for the elephant graveyard give the staircases a skeletal, serpentine look.

Elephant Graveyard

Richard Hudson designed the graveyard staircase in the same shape as Pride Rock, but its form is camouflaged by a covering of bones and riblike pieces. Like Pride Rock, this staircase spirals up from below the stage and is met with a freewheeling staircase that comes on from the wings. Together the units form a serpentine, skeletal spine that continually changes shape as the units revolve. This allows for the wild chase of little Simba and Nala by the hyenas.

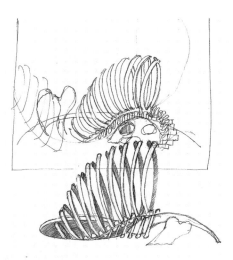

For the second scene in the elephant graveyard, the bone staircase on which Scar sings "Be Prepared" is cantilevered over the orchestra pit. This position thrusts Scar into the audience, and from there he cajoles the hyenas into arranging "the coup of the century." At this point black scrims descend over the white sych and side light boxes in order to create an ominous black void. Geysers of CO_2 steam shoot out of several traps in the deck. Thirty hyenas emerge from the pit, surge down the aisles, and take over the stage.

Opposite: The set models show the pattern on the floor as well as how the set functions.

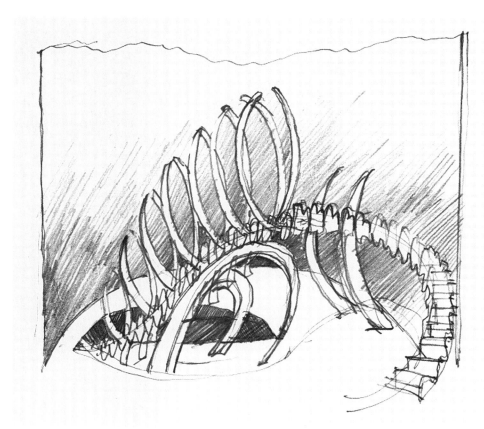

The set models shows the pattern on the floor as well as how the set functions.

The Stampede

To move quickly from the elephant graveyard and a stage full of rampaging hyenas to the canyons of the wildebeest stampede is one of the more hair-raising demands of this musical. Out of necessity, and because I am partial to nonverbal moments, we conceived what is known as a cover scene that happens downstage while the scene change is taking place upstage behind a giant shadow screen. Small shadow puppets of Simba and Scar journey along in silhouette, while downstage, two full-scale giraffes saunter by. The musical transition allows stagehands time to shift the set, and enables the audience to pause and cleanse its palate before the next action-packed scene. After a few minutes, the actors, Scar and Simba, enter and begin the dialogue that leads into the stampede.

The shift from an open, expansive scene to a shallow, intimate one is again a way to use cinematic techniques theatrically. In quiet moments, or when the audience needs to hear dialogue, scenes are pulled downstage in a kind of theatrical equivalent of a close-up. The audience can see the facial expressions of the characters in detail. Then, when the stage opens up again, as it does for the stampede, one feels the theatrical equivalent of a camera pulling back for a long shot.

Rehearsing with a shadow puppet of young Simba, for the sequence preceding the hair-raising wildebeest stampede.

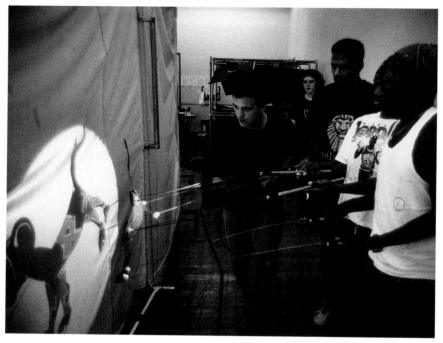

The wildebeest stampede takes place in a canyon formed by five sets of rust-colored portals that slide in from the wings and are located one behind the other, receding in false perspective. The idea is to convey the impression of herds of wildebeest running toward the audience from a long distance away. Miniature wildebeest, painted on a canvas roller drop, start to scroll downward at the back of the stage. From the ground between the canyon walls rises first one, then a second large roller dotted with miniature sculptures of more wildebeest. The rollers rotate like an old-fashioned penny arcade game, and create the sense of the herds careening toward the audience.

The Stampede

Creating the effect of hundreds of stampeding wildebeest on stage was a challenge. Richard Hudson devised the idea of a canvas scroll at the rear of the stage, painted with images of wildebeest, and in front of that rollers dotted with miniature models of wildebeest.

Following pages: As the scroll moves and the rollers turn, it seems as though wildebeest are pouring into the canyon. Dancers in wildebeest costumes, carrying giant masks, appear on stage to complete the illusion of animals rushing toward the audience.

The use of rollers to simulate the oncoming wildebeest harks back to 18th-century European theater, which often used rollers decorated with wavelike structures to create the effect of a sea. Placing side portals one behind the other to create false perspective goes back to the scenic designs of the Italian Renaissance, but it's a very simple method of making a canyon.

—*Richard Hudson,*
Scenic Designer

A line of stampeding dancers, each wearing three full-scale wildebeest masks, rises out of the stage-wide trap down in front of the rollers. Simba runs for his life, trying to stay ahead of them. Farthest downstage, a second row of stomping dancers emerges with even larger masks, five-foot shields with gigantic horns that thrust at the audience aggressively. Meanwhile, there are various perches high up on the canyon walls to give playing spaces for the principal characters. Underscoring the action are huge taiko drums that blast from the percussionists visibly situated in the theater's side boxes.

The scene is fraught with difficulty and split-second timing. Both Mufasa and Simba are harnessed for their action. Simba has to leap up and cling to the branch of a tree, then fall into the gorge. Mufasa, after putting his son out of danger, climbs 20 feet up the edge of the canyon wall and, with Scar's help, falls back into the midst of the wildebeest. It is the kind of scene that requires step-by-step planning and technical coordination during rehearsal, so that actors do not injure themselves and the staging flows smoothly.

There are not many technologically created sound effects in the show because most of the effects are being created by the orchestra and the percussive instruments. The wildebeest stampede is really the only substantial effect we are attempting, and even that is being supplemented by drums. What are known as subwoofers are installed in a space below the orchestra floor of the New Amsterdam and, if possible, below the seats in the two balconies. These large bass speakers accentuate sound and also vibrate, so that the audience both hears and feels the sensation of trampling hooves.

—*Tony Meola,*
Sound Designer

A wildebeest shield.

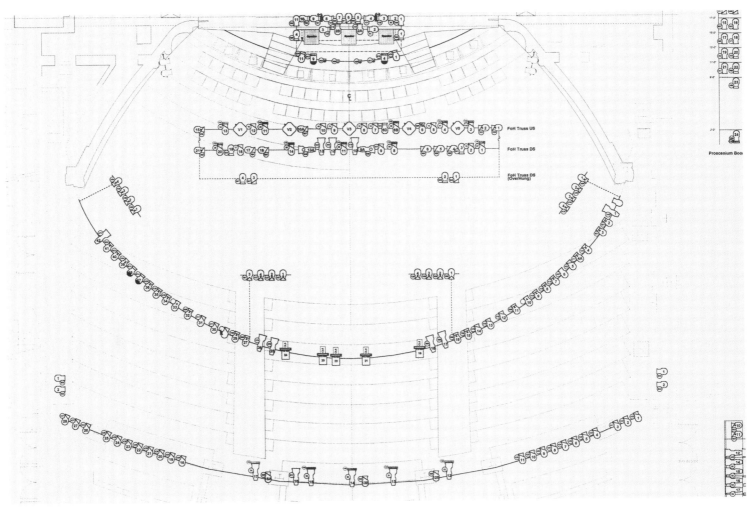

One of Donald Holder's lighting plots shows the placement of instruments.

For the lighting plot, I go through the show scene by scene, scenic moment by scenic moment, and decide how the scene will look from a lighting point of view. Then I go through the process of trying to achieve those ideas through the selection and placement of lighting instruments on a plan. I choose the kind of instruments and the color filters. On paper, the plot for *The Lion King* calls for 600 fixed lights and about 100 moving lights. Once rehearsals start, we learn what needs to be modified.

—*Donald Holder,
Lighting Designer*

The Jungle

At the end of Act One, the audience is introduced to Timon and Pumbaa, the savanna transforms into the jungle, and Simba ages eight years in eight seconds. To herald the new comic duo and the radically new environment, Richard designed inflatable greenery, giant cactuslike plants that blow up out of the

Richard Hudson's early design for the jungle set called for large banana leaves.

The first jungle set I designed used flat, 14-foot-long banana leaves. Lots of them. They were to be situated on each side of the stage, behind the "legs," and also above the stage, on the grid. When they appeared, they were to unfold like fans. But we had reservations about whether the design was abstract enough compared to the rest of the show, and so we decided upon long, branchless leaves that appear to be suspended in the air. The leaves are multilayered, and they can descend to give a dark, claustrophobic feeling, or be raised to give the stage an airier, lighter atmosphere. This design is capable of more variety than the first.

—*Richard Hudson,*
Scenic Designer

deck during the song "Hakuna Matata." I had wanted the jungle to be a playful environment, like a wild jungle gym, and the inflatable plants were a perfect solution for the beginning of the scenic transformation. They also could deflate on cue whenever the aromatic Pumbaa strode by.

In Act Two, most of the action takes place in the jungle, and it turned out that this was Richard's most challenging design. His first attempts were quite beautiful, enormous jungle leaves that tracked from the flies and offered many different configurations. The only problem was that all of a sudden the look was too literal, that the minimalist gestures of the first act had given way to a more realisic, storybook approach. Finally, between the two of us, we came up with a concept that seemed to be in keeping with the style we had set. Richard designed layers of hanging drops of invisible net that had translucent green silk streamers attached to them. These "vines" or dashes of leaves create a

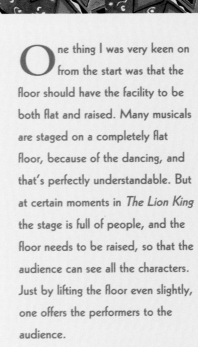

labyrinthine depth and can either fill the space or hang as a bower high above it. The simplicity of the pattern of green brush strokes is a perfect balance to the detail of the characters who inhabit the stage.

It was my task to design costumes that presented varied foliage and flowers of the paradise presented in "Can You Feel the Love Tonight." As in Act One with the grasslands chorus, I wanted to create moving, breathing scenery worn and operated by the performers themselves. As the song unfolds, the jungle landscape comes alive. Flowers blossom. Entwined dancers rise from plants and descend from the flies like floating vines. As the teenage Simba and Nala walk through this world, the costumes of the chorus reveal lush, fanning leaves and petals, and the scene's color transmutes from green to fuschia to golden yellows and oranges.

Richard Hudson's second approach to the jungle was more abstract, in keeping with the vision for the rest of the production.

Costume renderings for the luxurious
plants and flowers that bloom and cavort during
"Can You Feel the Love Tonight."

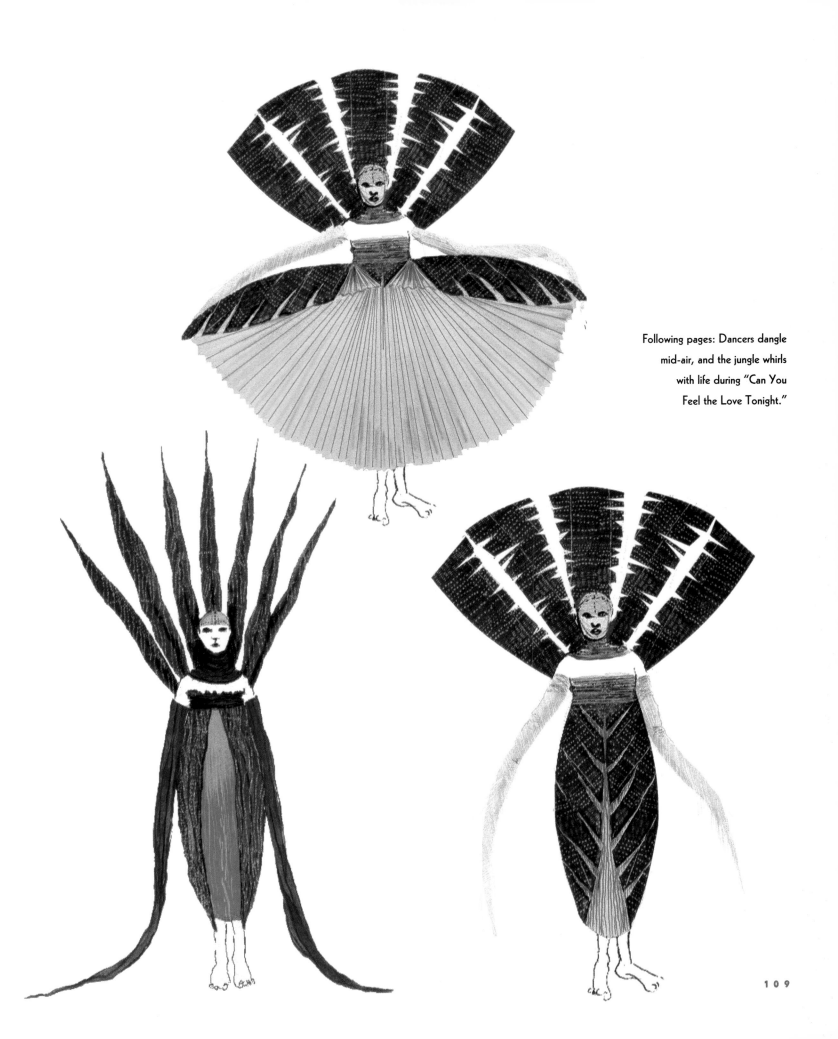

Following pages: Dancers dangle
mid-air, and the jungle whirls
with life during "Can You
Feel the Love Tonight."

A scene titled "Simba's Nightmare" involves one of the more complicated scenic designs of Act Two. The waterfall was conceived as an image of danger for the sequence where Simba relives the stampede and his father's death. First, a river represented by a four-foot-wide strip of long silk is stretched across the stage. As two dancers undulate the silk, colorful shadow puppets of fish move behind it. The puppets glide across the stage on pallets, each equipped with its own light source. Simba, who has led his friends to the riverside, easily leaps over the river. Taunted by Simba, Timon tries to jump across, but his short legs make it impossible for him to reach the other side. He falls into the river and is carried offstage.

Shadow puppets of fish are visible behind a four-foot-wide strip of silk, the river which little Timon vainly tries to leap during "Simba's Nightmare."

Immediately, a waterfall drops out of the sky. After much deliberation, Don, Richard, and I decided to go with a combination of moving silk (the classic, naive approach), CO_2 fog, and very simple moving projections of an African textile design. The combination of techniques kept the illusion from being either too flat or too slick and realistic.

A miniature, mechanized Timon puppet comes shooting over the fall and grasps a branch, just as little Simba does during the stampede. The diminutive size of this puppet accentuates the grand scale of the waterfall and allows our human actor time to travel under the stage to prepare for his imminent emergence from the pool. The sound of the thundering waterfall transforms into drumming wildebeest hooves, and as Timon screams for help, Simba freezes, and the image of a falling Mufasa mask appears through the cascading silk

Opposite: Drawings of dancers costumed like sinuous vines for "Can You Feel the Love Tonight."

1 1 3

Swept offstage by the river's current, Timon next appears as a miniature puppet at the top of the waterfall, while two crocodile puppets at the fall's base eagerly await Timon's descent. The illusion of furiously cascading water is created by billowing silk in combination with fog and projections of moving patterns of dots.

water. Unable to hold on any longer, the tiny Timon puppet tumbles into the "water" below and disappears, while snapping crocodiles emerge from the trap in the stage. Simba remains frozen until Timon, the actor, comes bounding out of the water via the elevator lift in the trap.

The Finale: Simba Confronts Scar

During the developmental process, one of the greatest challenges was how to stage the physically dramatic finale. In the film, one sees Simba's climb up the steep cliff, his slip off the edge, the battle of hyenas and lionesses, Scar's long fall, the lightning and subsequent inferno, and the final rains that cleanse and renew the ravaged landscape. A tall order for theater. The designers and I talked a great deal about the possible overuse of Pride Rock and the difficulty of staging a convincing fall. We talked about ringing Pride Rock with fire and creating a wall of rain as in the film, but both proved not only cost prohibitive but dangerous.

In order to suggest the constantly shifting perspective and locale I decided to use a moving shadow screen to counterpoint the fight choreography that Garth would create. Richard designed a giant shadow-puppet screen in the shape and color of Pride Rock, manipulated by the eight performers and lit from behind by puppeteers holding individual lights. The screen would enter and hide Pride Rock as it descended into the floor, leaving the entire stage free for the expansive choreography. The moving screen would whip around in a serpentine manner to reveal dancers or actors one moment and intricately carved shadow puppets the next. With the handheld battery lights, the shadows could rapidly shift scale.

The long-awaited confrontation between Simba (Jason Raize) and Scar (John Vickery).

We had prepared various shadow puppets to stage the difficult fights and falls between Scar and Simba. Ultimately, however, in rehearsal, with the collaboration of the actors, we decided to try to stage the dangerous confrontations between the live actors on top of Pride Rock and the moving staircase from the elephant graveyard. The shadow puppets seemed too removed to represent our principal characters and were useful only in creating a dynamic atmosphere of the melee.

An array of shadow puppets. They cast a delicate shadow when a light shines on them from behind, but they are made of a tough plastic called Lexan.

THE WORKSHOPS

The spring of development culminated in the summer's workshop and presentation. In addition to designing a raft of costumes, puppets, masks, and sets, we presented significant script changes. Brand-new elements included the change of gender for Rafiki, and the humorous new song and scene, "The Madness of King Scar." We also presented the lyrics I had written for "Endless Night," and those written for "Shadowland" by Mark Mancina and Lebo M.

In the two weeks allotted, the main emphasis was on the book and songs of the musical. The presentation was divided into two parts: a sit-down reading and a prototype demonstration of some of the key mask and puppet concepts.

Though the reading wasn't to include blocking, it was paramount during the rehearsal process to create some of the scenes on our feet, especially the more physical or confrontational moments. Also, there were some scenes that were created from scratch as well as certain visual ideas that were scratched once the actors entered the game. Lebo developed an African chant for the lioness hunt with the small chorus of twelve, paving the way for the future choreography of Garth. And the presence of South African Tsidii Le Loka in the role of Rafiki inspired a whole new approach to her first scene at the tree. Richard had designed a miniature globe that would spin, and Rafiki was to be the magical shaman that made the rain fall or the sun rise around that globe. However, as soon as Tsidii began improvising Zulu stories in her native tongue about the change of seasons, I knew the visual image of the globe should go. The performer was far more engaging and said it all.

The reading went extremely well, as did the presentation of set models, costume designs, and maquettes. The prototype portion of the workshop, however, revealed that some of the concepts clearly worked, while others were hard to gauge in such unfinished and under-rehearsed form. Response to the Pumbaa and hyena designs was positive, but for a variety of reasons the other prototypes drew less enthusiastic reactions. With only a few days of rehearsal, the actors did not have enough time to work with the puppets and masks to get by the technical difficulties.

In addition, the prototypes were white, unpainted models, and only the most minimal of costume pieces were worn. While the unfinished look did not

The vivacious Tsidii Le Loka played Rafiki in the August workshop and went on to the Broadway production.

The hyena was a certified hit at the August workshop.

Opposite page: After the August workshop, it was decided that a puppet version of Zazu would be more effective than a mask. Michael Curry's precise drawings break down the components for the mechanical Zazu puppet and illustrate the major animation features: the separate and flexible head extends out from the body of the puppet, and a wing apparatus allows one trigger to both open and flap the wings.

impede the audience's appreciation of Pumbaa or the hyena, it did interfere with the success of some of the other prototypes. The audience sat in a brightly lit studio, a mere ten feet from the actors, making illusion impossible to create.

The actor playing and manipulating Timon is intended to wear a green leaf-textured costume with accompanying green face makeup, which becomes a background to the terra-cotta color of the puppet Timon. Not only was the audience too close, but there was no lighting to guide the focus. In the flat, two-dimensional medium of film, the viewer focuses on most of the on-screen action at once. In the three-dimensional world of theater, the viewer hones in on the character in the foreground or where the lighting directs the audience to look. Though the actor playing Timon was quite wonderful, he had such little time with this new technique that, out of nerves, he tended to upstage the puppet, causing the focus to be split.

Michael Curry and I discovered immediately that the animatronic masks for Scar and Mufasa would not work as designed because they did not move along with the head of the actor. It was disconcerting to watch an actor's head move but see the mask stay still. We liked the animatronic masks in principle, but realized that each would have to be redesigned to move in tandem with the performer's head.

Mufasa's mask had moving eyes and eyebrows. While that lent more expression to the mask, ultimately the moving parts seemed extraneous. They undercut the mask's power and mystery, making it distractingly banal and busy. The actor's own face could provide the necessary facial expressions, while the masks, as in traditional mask theater, would seem to change expression by how the actor moves.

Zazu didn't work at all. The actor, who was terrifically charming in the reading, just seemed awkward and too big in the costume design I had created.

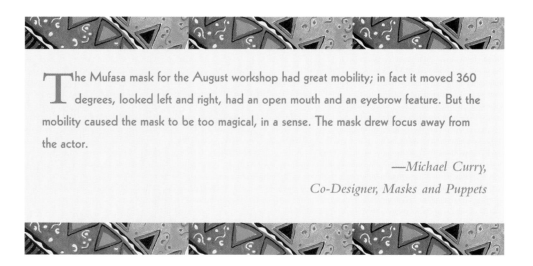

The Mufasa mask for the August workshop had great mobility; in fact it moved 360 degrees, looked left and right, had an open mouth and an eyebrow feature. But the mobility caused the mask to be too magical, in a sense. The mask drew focus away from the actor.

—Michael Curry,
Co-Designer, Masks and Puppets

It was quite clear that the small scale of the hornbill was important and that we should go back to thinking about a puppet version of this character.

Because the reading went smoothly, more focus was placed on the prototypes. One of the questions asked by the producers was whether the principal characters should be animals equipped with puppets and masks, or human beings with stylized makeup and wigs. Perhaps only the chorus should be the more extremely designed mask and puppet animals. These questions led us to schedule a second workshop early in 1997 for the purpose of deciding these issues.

There was little question, however, that the script, music, and performances held together. While visual design is fundamental, the book and the score have to carry the show, and we felt at the end of this part of the process that *The Lion King* would work as a stage musical.

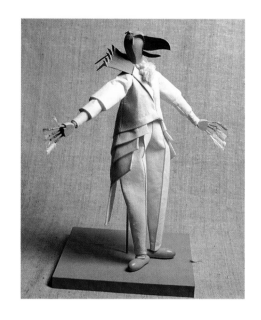

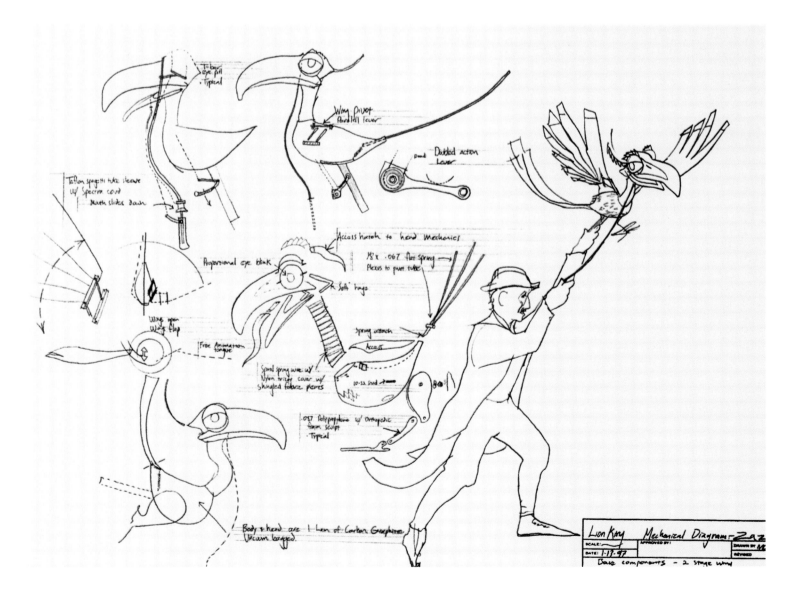

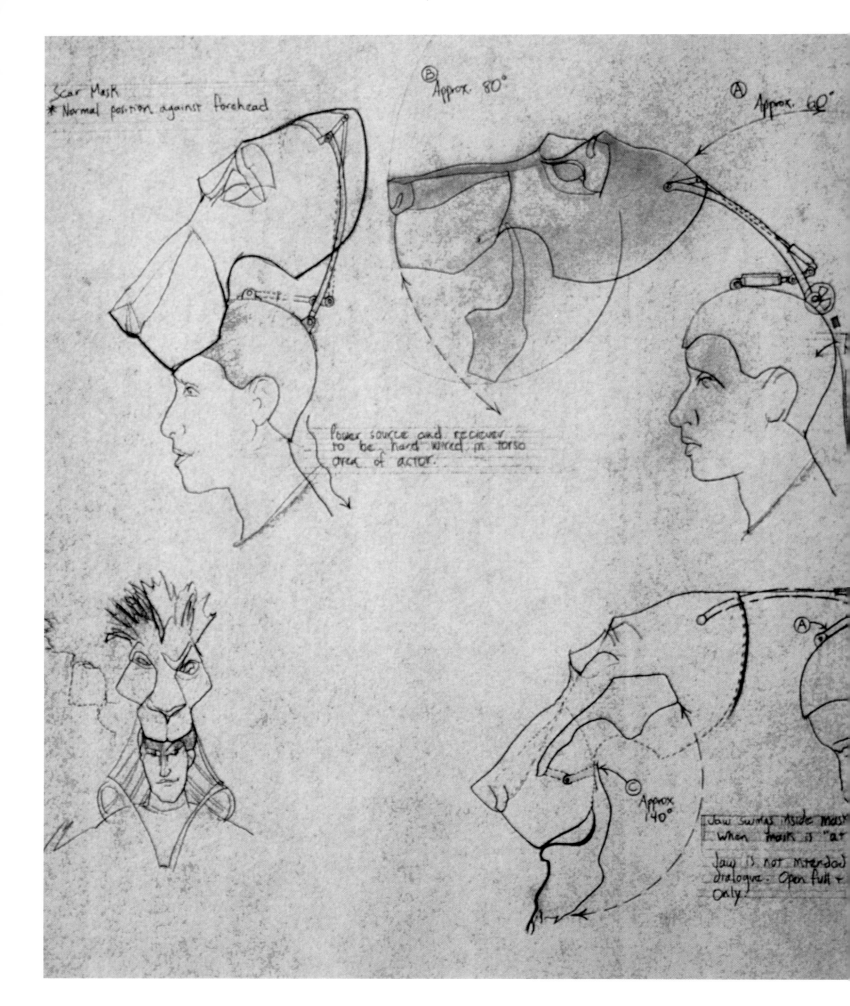

Scar Mask
* Normal position against forehead

Ⓑ Approx. 80°

Ⓐ Approx. 60°

Power source and reciever
to be hard wired in torso
area of actor.

Ⓐ

Ⓒ Approx
40°

Jaw swings inside mask
when mask is "at
Jaw is not intended
dialogue. Open full +
only.

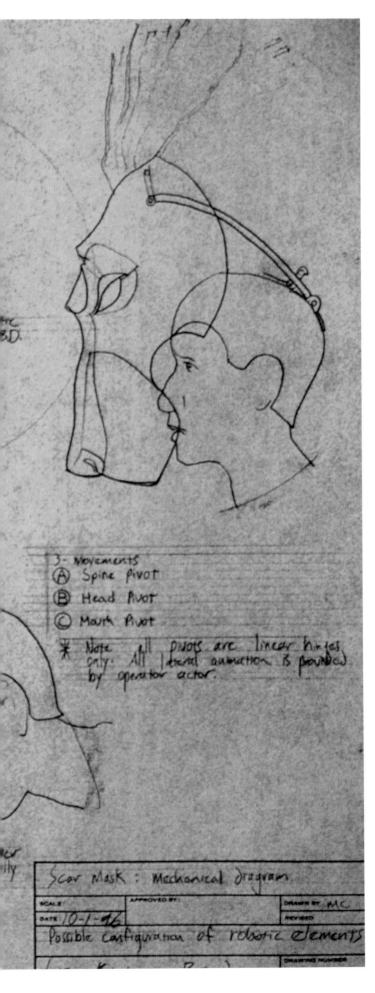

Michael Curry demonstrates how Scar's mask rises up and extends in front of the performer's head.

Far left: Michael Curry's drawings for Scar's animatronic mask show the mask's range of motion in relation to an actor's head. Michael takes the silhouette of the mask and the silhouette of the actor's head and finds the pattern of movement—the extension—he wants, and then he scales it to find the length of the mechanical struts that will achieve the desired range. Scar's mask has an extension of 22 inches.

My father and grandfather were loggers in Oregon, and loggers are the most amazing engineers. So it seemed natural for me to build things. I studied engineering as well as fine arts, both of which feed into the building and designing of masks and puppets.

—Michael Curry,
Co-Designer,
Masks and Puppets

The February '97 meeting at the New Amsterdam was one of the most important artistic breakthroughs in the process of bringing Julie's vision to life and the characters to the stage. Julie's concept of portraying the "double event," as she calls it, of showing both the human and the animal, could only be realized by going into a theater space and trying it. Months of struggle and creativity were poured into those two weeks and it was nothing short of exhilarating to see her concept begin to take real life.

—*Thomas Schumacher*

February 1997

In a sense, the pre-production phase of *The Lion King* began within months of the August presentation. As we addressed the issue of whether the main characters should be human beings in stylized makeup or the animal/human double event, we started taking bids from various shops that would build scenery and costumes, design a sound system, and provide lighting.

I vowed that any future prototype demonstrations would present finished costumes, puppets, masks, and full makeup, and would take place on a fully lit stage, with people watching from an appropriate distance. We began to prepare for two weeks of rehearsal, which would culminate in a prototype presentation at the New Amsterdam Theater on February 10.

To address the question of human versus animal, we decided to stage selections from two scenes: the musical's first scene of dialogue, during which Scar threatens Zazu and Mufasa; and "Hakuna Matata," the scene and song during which Pumbaa and Timon come upon little Simba in the desert. Each scene would be done twice: once with puppets or masks, and once with costumes and makeup only. In preparation for the workshop we were able to rework Scar's mask, finish the details of the Timon puppet, and construct a Zazu puppet. We also built the costumes for the three characters. And in the cases of Timon and Zazu, we recast for actors who had not only the acting skills but the physical skills necessary for the techniques.

Michael Curry returned to his Oregon studio to focus on the masks and puppets. He ended up devising an animatronic mask for Scar that rests firmly on the actor's head. Made out of carbon graphite, it weighs only 31 ounces—less than a motorcycle helmet. Not only does it align with the actor's head, but it can be controlled easily by pressing a lever worn on the hand. Meanwhile, we downscaled the Scar mask to avoid overshadowing the actor's face. And for the costume/makeup version of that character, Michael Ward designed a spiky-looking headdress that complemented the bonyness of the rest of his costume.

While considering an alternative for the Timon puppet, I began to see the character as a commedia dell'arte figure, a cunning if not always smart Harlequino. Keeping in mind the physique of a meerkat, I designed a costume that conveys the animal's shape, giving it narrow ankles and a long, low waist. The pattern of the fabric was a cross between Harlequino motley and African

TAYMOR

patch design. The actor would wear a piece mask on his face allowing for partial facial expression while helping to form his own features into those of Timon.

A bird puppet was built for Zazu. This rod puppet, with its comically flexi-

A possible alternative to the Timon puppet:
a costume in commedia dell'arte style.

The Zazu puppet receives a coat of paint by Liza Pastine prior to the prototype presentation.

ble neck, blinking eyelids, and movable beak, is one of the production's most traditional puppets. I decided that the originally designed formal blue tailcoat and bowler hat would work whether we ended up using the puppet or the actor. For the purely human version, however, Zazu would have long feathery fingers and makeup that would highlight his face.

I had no objection to staging these scenes utilizing the alternative techniques because I saw it as a true advantage in working out the kinks of our experimental designs. Though I knew the new and improved pieces would definitely work better than the August prototypes, I tried to keep my mind open to the success of either concept. If the actor versions were more moving or engaging, then it was fine with me. There was no doubt in my mind that the production could work either way. Deep down, however, Michael and I rooted for the more extreme and unique approaches.

We rehearsed for almost two weeks, and every day it seemed that a puppet or mask needed an adjustment. The Timon puppet needed to be taken apart so that its midsection could be made more flexible. The rods on the Zazu puppet were too long for the actor, who had difficulty holding them and squeezing the mechanisms that open the beak and shutter the eyelids. Every time the Scar mask retracted from its extended, lunging position, it hit the actor in the face. It was hell on the actors as they tried to keep sane about being guinea pigs in our grand experiment. Each day Michael Curry's assistants trooped from the shop to the rehearsal studio, tenderly carrying puppets and masks back and forth for mending or reworking.

Watching the actors rehearse with the puppets, I saw their potential, but I worried. I began to wonder if we were becoming too conscious of the artifice, too aware of the technique. Would the puppetry interfere with telling the story? But whenever one of the actors began to master the form, I felt the tremendous emotion that a puppet or mask can communicate. I watched Scar and knew that a human being alone could not achieve the same visual power without the mask. The interplay between the performer and his extended animal character was new and exciting.

A prototype demonstration like the one at the New Amsterdam is a theatrical hybrid. For the actors, it has all the pressures of a performance. They spend hours in dressing rooms while Michael Ward puts on their makeup and wigs, and then they are helped into complex costumes and masks. They have pre-performance jitters. For the small group of executives at the New Amsterdam, however, the purpose was not to assess the quality of acting and singing but rather the technique we would use to portray the characters. Does the Zazu puppet, a white bird with orange and blue tailfeathers, communicate the vast range of expressions, and what is the interaction between the puppet and the actor manipulating him? Do the green wig, makeup, and costume worn by the actor playing Timon distract from the puppet he is operating? How does his costume/makeup version look next to the Pumbaa puppet? Can the Scar costume, with its spiky headdress, hold the stage as well as the animatronic mask combined with the actor? Which versions are more fun and challenging?

Ultimately, the producers' fears about focus in the puppet/mask alternatives were allayed. Though the viewer was completely aware both of the human being and the animal, the singular essence of the characters came through, much more so than when the scenes were performed in a more traditional way, with the actors in costume and makeup only.

Scar's spikey wig, at one point an alternative to the mask.

A bit of directorial duty during the February workshop.

Above: Sharing a moment with
Michael Eisner.

Right: Max Casella as Timon and
Tom Robbins as Pumbaa.

As Michael Eisner pointed out, the more difficult and unusual approach of using puppets and masks is the bigger risk. But the artistic reward promises to be bigger as well.

Opposite page: Geoff Hoyle and the Zazu puppet strike an elegant pose.

ACT III

PERFORMANCE

THE END OF THE FEBRUARY WORKSHOP marked the beginning of an intensive drive toward opening night. The collaborative atmosphere that infused the development process does not evaporate when director and designers shift their attention to this final, critical stage. But everyone returns to their own tasks, each designer digging in for the last push. The main shop is alive with builders creating puppets and masks. Michael Curry travels back and forth between his shops in Oregon and New York City. Richard Hudson, now back in England, has his associate designer, Peter Eastman, and the technical director, David Benken, oversee the construction of the sets in the various shops in the United States and Canada. Tony Meola and Don Holder put together their respective sound and lighting packages. Mary Peterson and Tracy Dorman work with me visiting the various costume shops and individual dyers, painters, and craftsmen to begin the preparation of fabrics for the costumes. Most of the costumes cannot be built until the show is cast and the measurements of the actors can be taken.

Left: Soldering is among the tasks at Hudson Scenic Studio, Inc., where some of the scenery for *The Lion King* was built. Above: Studying a model of the staircase for the elephant graveyard with Assistant Director Dan Fields.

Opposite page: Contemplating a bird headdress with Michael Curry.

Taking in the enormity of the elephant graveyard staircase at Hudson Scenic Studio.

I f *The Lion King* were a conventional production, one that required men's suits and women's dresses, the costume shops would begin doing what is known as swatching fabrics: showing the designer samples of cloth. But many of the fabrics in *The Lion King* are custom-painted, printed, or dyed, so that the production will have as authentically African a look as possible (the fabric for Zazu's blue tailcoat was originally blankets). In many cases, the fabric is made to order, rather than cut from bolts of cloth.

As soon as the production is cast, actors are measured for their costumes and, working from the costume maquettes, the shops start building muslins, or fabric patterns. When rehearsals start, fittings begin in earnest, and the completed costumes are delivered to the theater in time for technical and dress rehearsals.

—*Mary Peterson,*
Associate Costume Designer

Christianne Myers (top) and Elea Crowther (above) carefully paint fabric for the costumes of the singing lionesses at Joni Johns' studio.
Right: Fabric painter Mary Macy hand-paints a gazelle body suit.
Opposite page, clockwise from top left:
Artist Joan Morris, who used a sophisticated dyeing technique called *shibori* to create the vivid colors of the jungle costume; Associate Costume Designer Mary Peterson considers the length of a silk glove for a jungle costume; Marisela Campos attending to a grasslands costume at Parsons-Meares; skirts barely swing as the stately grasslands chorus proceeds across the stage.

CASTING

As director, casting the show became my primary concern. Of the thirteen principal roles, seven of the actors who had participated in the August or February workshops were asked to be in the production. Obviously this was a terrific advantage. We would know, to a degree, what we would be getting, and the actors would have a jump-start on their parts. They would also know what they were getting into. The last six roles took four to five months to cast. The criteria for the principals was to look for actors who act, sing, and move well—not a small order. During auditions, it is also vital for me to imagine what an actor will look like wearing a mask. Is the shape of the head powerful enough to carry the design?

I also brought puppets to auditions to see how performers would look in relation to specific puppets and how they would respond when asked to animate an inanimate object. And though performers would not be totally immersed within the puppets nor hidden behind the masks, they would have to be willing to accept that the audience is not going to be looking at them alone. Attitude is a very important part of my casting decision. I want an actor who is going to enjoy the challenge and not view it as a burden.

Rather than expressly hiring puppeteers, I look for inventive actors who move well. A strong actor gives an idiosyncratic performance, because he infuses the puppet character with his own personality instead of relying on generic puppetry technique. The thrill of working with a good actor who is new to this medium, and who loves the puppet he is working with, is that he will take the form further than I ever imagined.

Of the 27-member chorus, we sought 12 dancers and 15 singers. Once again a few of the singers who had done the workshop were invited into the company but the majority was left to cast. It was a very tricky affair. Lebo M wanted at least half of the chorus to be South African. A number of the songs were in Zulu or had a strong South African chant underscore. This style of singing is so distinct that it cannot be learned but

Max Casella learns to manipulate the Timon puppet.

As a director, Julie is very interactive. She allows—sometimes insists—that the actors bring ideas into the rehearsal room, that they develop moments and business. And she responds instantaneously to what they bring in. If she loves something, she'll say, "That's great, keep it, keep it.'"

At the same time, when she has something in mind that she's trying to achieve, she's very eager to get to it. I don''t think she knows how an actor is exactly supposed to fulfill a specific moment— she allows the performer to discover that. But she definitely has a specific idea about how a scene builds, how it moves and flows and where the dramatic punctuation is. And she relies on the actors to find ways to make those things happen.

The actors spent less time reading the script out loud with each other than I've seen in many productions. *The Lion King* is such a human story, and it involves so much physicalization, mostly through masks and puppetry but also through the actors' bodies, that the actors had to get on their feet right away. We started with a discussion, and then we worked the scenes with the principal characters: their book scenes, their music scenes and movement, adding in the puppets and the masks and working with that intensely, and then we brought in the chorus. At that point, Julie sat everyone down and explained what was going to happen on stage, showed them the costume renderings and set designs again, reminded them what the look and the tone of a scene were, what we were all trying to achieve.

It is an inclusive process, and Julie relies not just on the principals but on everybody to use their imaginations. The difference between a person just walking around in a zebra costume, and an actor who imbues that puppet with a physicalization, has to do with Julie making the performer realize that he or she is a part of the process.

The fourth week of rehearsal, she had everybody come into the main rehearsal room to work on the final scene for the first time. She sat them down and basically acted out the scene for them. She explained all the different components and got so excited that the company could not help but feel excited with her.

She comes into the room with all of her designs and concepts and ideas for how things are going to work out, but really opens her arms to the performers and asks for their creativity.

—Dan Fields,
Assistant Director

only imitated and all of us were determined to have an authentic sound for our musical. Actor's Equity conceded to six South African performers whom Lebo handpicked. Added to the South African contingent were Lebo and his wife, Nandi, leaving seven choral spots open. Even trickier at this point was the hard fact that understudies for all of the principal roles would have to come from the chorus. This is no easy task even for the most straightforward musical, but it is particularly challenging in *The Lion King* because the principal roles require a completely different set of skills from the chorus. We agreed to hire two full-time covers for the roles of Scar, Timon, Pumbaa, and Zazu. And the two child roles would each have his and her own understudy.

While casting the dancers I caught my first glimpse at the type of choreography Garth would bring to the piece. What I saw was athletic, sexy, rhythmically complex, and perfect for what I had envisioned. Four hundred dancers showed up for the open female dance call in New York. Quite clearly Mr. Fagan was a draw. Garth's auditions were murderous. His two terrific assistants, performers from his own company, would demonstrate a routine and the dancers would do their best to learn it. Sometimes these routines were two or three minutes long and had to be instantly memorized. I asked Garth why he made the audition so difficult and he said that he wanted not only to see if a dancer had good technique but also to see how fast he or she could learn. He wanted to let them know what they would be in for.

NEW YORK REHEARSALS

We plannned to rehearse five weeks in New York and spend three weeks in technical rehearsals, on stage, in Minneapolis for our out-of-town tryout. The first day of rehearsal is totally nerve-racking and thrilling. We had about a hundred people in the room for the reading and presentation of the scenic, puppet and costume designs. Everyone from the Disney theatrical office and the puppet shop was invited. Gathered around an immense table, the actors read through the script and stumbled their way through the songs. The concept was laid out for the company, the goal set before them, and we were ready to begin.

At our studio at 890 Broadway we had four large rooms in which to do our work: one for music and choral rehearsals with Lebo and Joe; one for dance

The first day of rehearsal was like the first day of school. People were anxious, excited, and scared. Some people knew each other—they were the ones hugging. Others didn't know anybody, and were worried about that. Some knew that there had been a lot of work done, because they went for a puppet fitting four days earlier and saw all the puppets and knew that people had been thinking about this production. But others were worried because they *hadn't* been to a fitting. Some worried about being good enough. Those emotions ran rampant in the room that morning. But after six months of rehearsals and performances, everyone will be on the same page.

—*Peter Schneider*

with Garth; the main room for scene rehearsals with me; and a puppet hospital where the masks and puppets could be stored, repaired, and actors could work and experiment individually on their own in front of mirrors or with the aid of videotape. Every day the assistant directors and artistic team would spend our lunch hour agonizing and organizing the most complicated rehearsal schedule designed to take advantage of everyone at every moment. With more than two hundred intricate costume designs, the individual fittings also had to be worked into the daily schedule.

PRINCIPAL REHEARSALS

During the first rehearsal days I worked improvisationally with the principal actors. We would move back and forth between reading and analyzing the text and getting up on our feet and improvising with both the text and the physical relationships of the characters. The masks and puppets were built, if not completely painted, by the time we went into rehearsal, and I urged the performers to wear or use them as much as possible. It is misleading for an actor to think he can find his or her character without the puppet or mask, especially in the case of Timon or Zazu, where the character is actually a complete puppet that is manipulated by the actor. Quite often, though, in discovering the natural flow of a scene or the more human gestures and inner nuances that might arise from the unencumbered performer, I would ask the actors to play the scenes without their "extended parts." The fun began when they then had to find the corresponding animal gestures through the vocabulary of the puppets and masks.

At this early stage I asked performers to find "ideograghs" for their characters. An ideograph is a concept that I was first exposed to during the late 1960s, while I was studying mime with Jacques LeCoq at his L'Ecole de Mime in Paris. The concept was applied again during the 1970s, when I was a member of The Oberlin Group in Ohio, an experimental theater troupe led by avant-garde director Herbert Blau. In the visual arts, an example of an ideograph would be a Japanese brush painting of a bamboo forest: Just three or four quick brush strokes capture the whole. In the theater, an ideograph is also a pared-down form—a kinetic, abstract essence of an emotion, an action, or a

There have been two highlights for me. The first was the reading in August 1996, when I heard new voices shape the material and new songs and music added in. And the second highlight was the first day of rehearsals. Looking out at the cast and seeing those faces, hearing the show sung through, seeing the fragments of the designs—it was absolutely thrilling to me. I was stunned. Because the theater can be a bit cynical, and the wide-eyed willingness to engage in such a non-traditional process and non-traditional piece, with a non-traditional cast, was overwhelming to me. We have made choices that, although risky, seem the right thing to have done.

—*Thomas Schumacher*

character. At L'Ecole de Mime, LeCoq enjoined us to create ideographs of colors and materials, to "do red," "do blue," "be ice," or "be steel." We used our bodies to create ideographic images of the sun setting or of melting snow fields. We also explored ideographs of emotions. The idea was not to imitate ice or steel or joy but to reveal the essential kernel of the subject without the distracting details. A haiku.

I use ideographs in various ways in all aspects of my theater work. Once in rehearsal, I use the technique to help an actor find and express the essence of a character. The actor playing Pumbaa suggested during rehearsal that the ideograph for the fat, waddling warthog was "contentment," and he expressed this physically by just standing in one spot and breathing in a full, relaxed way. Timon, on the other hand, is a nervous, street-wise meerkat, and so his ideograph might be related to canniness or toughness. Again, the performer would not act out toughness, but rather find an essential, abstract series of movements

John Vickery, Geoff Hoyle, and Sam Wright rehearse the scene in which Scar defies Mufasa.

On stage, Scar (John Vickery)
and Mufasa (Sam Wright)
fearlessly confront each other.

Clockwise from top left: Sam Wright, Jason Raize, and Heather Headley are fitted for costumes at Barbara Matera, Ltd., in New York.

which embody that character trait. These exercises lead the actor toward finding a physical, spatial, and rhythmic score for his character.

I often use ideographs to open up a text's visual motifs and themes. For my staging of *Titus Andronicus,* Shakespeare's most graphically bloody tragedy, actors explored ideographs for violence, racism, the meaning of the sacred and profane. In any theater piece requiring heightened style, ideographs can be used to find the physical vocabulary that matches the language, or in the case of *The Lion King,* that matches the style of the music and the overall nature of the production.

The dialogue in *The Lion King* is conversational, but from the design to the score, the piece is highly stylized. Each actor had to find the duality of the animal and the human within their performance. An actress cannot put on Nala's mask and costume and talk with Simba as though she had just run into him on the street. As lioness/young woman she has to find a way of standing, walking and gesturing that fulfills the demands of the production's conceit. The tension inherent in the juxtaposition of the highly stylized gestural moves with the more naturalistic ones was my main thrust in the direction of the actors. Complete stylization would have been too formal and distancing for the audience, and would not service the script. The audience needs to identify with the characters, to recognize in them their selves, and therefore the familiar landscapes of emotion, dialogue, and interaction needed to be partially expressed in a familiar way. If the entire piece were performed naturalistically these moments would not stand out. In fact, the audience would take the most recognizable gestures for granted. What makes these simple human moments powerful is the selected isolation of them and the contrast and interplay with the heightened or stylized forms of expression.

Once the actors have their masks, they use their bodies to complete the sculpture. The architectural flow of the mask is the map or guide. Scar's mask is twisted and angular. John Vickery had to continue that angularity with his body. The stylized costume I designed obviously helps, but the actor must find his own rhythmic and spatial complement. When wearing a mask, an actor's head movements must be precise, strong, and clean. As the mask has no interior facial expression it is the way the actor isolates the head and body that gives the illusion of change.

Simba (Jason Raize) and Nala (Heather Headley) share a tender moment in Act II.

Scar (John Vickery) talks sternly
to a frightened young Simba
(Scott Irby-Ranniar).

One of the keys to puppetry is stillness. Too much movement from a puppet forces the physicality to become general and unfocused. The actor must learn to make quick, small moves that contrast with long, luxurious ones, and to alternate motion with stasis. The individual movements become the pauses, the commas and the exclamation points in the character's phrasing. At the same time, energy levels must remain high and consistent. If an actor's kinetic intensity drops, the puppet loses energy. As the puppet Timon was explored we found that we needed to develop different mechanisms to keep every limb vital. While Max Cassela had his right hand articulating the mouth of the puppet and his left hand manipulating the left arm of the puppet, a holder was strapped to his right thigh which, when moved, allowed him to animate the right arm of the puppet. The challenge for the actor was to bring his puppet to life—to get "blood" flowing into every digit, into the legs, into the head, so that the audience sees and feels the life force inside this inanimate object.

When a figure made of wood or fabric moves like a living thing, the visual and emotional impact is magical. Watching puppetry at its best is a cubistic event, because an audience experiences the art from several perspectives at once. One can either focus solely on the puppet or enjoy the direct and transparent art of the actor motivating that puppet. At rest, a puppet is just a facsimile of a human being or an animal. But when Zazu's wings flutter excitedly or Timon cocks his head at a quizzical angle, the pleasure of watching that facsimile turn into a being with recognizable emotions is the pinnacle of this type of theater experience.

During rehearsal, Kajuana Shuford
crouches behind Geoff Hoyle, while
Scott Irby-Ranniar, playing young Simba,
tries to stare down two hyenas,
Shenzi (Tracy Nicole Chapman) and
Banzai (Stanley Wayne Mathis).

Pumbaa (Tom Robbins) and Timon (Max Casella) jubilantly welcome young Simba (Scott Irby-Ranniar) to their life of "Hakuna Matata."

Following pages: Ribbons of tears fall from the lionesses as they mourn the dead Mufasa (Sam Wright).

CHOREOGRAPHY

Prior to rehearsals Garth and I had laid out when dance would serve as the main event of a scene, or in a musical number, and at what points I would need him to work with the principals on their choreography. Herds and flocks of animals needed to lope, leap, fly, and stampede. The flora needed to blossom and blow in the wind. Songs simply needed kinetic respite from the lyrical sections. Some of these stagings were a joyous collaboration between Garth, the actors,

I want the choreography to look unlike typical Broadway dancing. I want the dance to look like an integral part of this community, of this *Lion King* land. Of course *Lion King* land includes strong elements from Africa, so that means body-rhythmic and weighted movement, the kind of movement used by cultures that are close to the earth and to nature. I want dance in which fantastic, unusual patterns and shapes evolve, shapes of dancers' bodies, shapes of unions of dancers. Some shapes are related to the African base of the piece, and some are just magical.

There are challenges. How do you stage a hunt of lionesses without imitating the animal, but still get across the tenacity of the hunt? What are the elements of a lioness hunt that human bodies can depict? One of the things that intrigued me most when I saw a pride of lions in Kenya was a lion's huge, powerful shoulders, which come at you when they move. That's an important image that I want to capture and maintain.

In "Can You Feel the Love Tonight," I have to get across an understanding of love in its broadest terms, and that involves choreographing couples on different levels and having dancers emerge from unexpected places on the stage. On the other hand, a dance number like "I Can't Wait to Be King" is just joyous, and every child in the audience understands that, and the children within us grown-ups respond to it as well. A child saying, "I just can't wait until you're not around to boss me anymore" is universal. It exists in every culture.

Perhaps most importantly, the dance numbers should seem to come out of nowhere and surprise the audience, and then dissipate like emphemeral dreams, instead of telegraphing themselves with big wind-ups and then closing with equally big wind-downs.

—*Garth Fagan,*
Choreographer

and myself, but most of the dance choreography was created in Garth's workroom. In reality, Garth had the least amount of time to rehearse because everything he was creating was from scratch, while the music and text had already been written and had been tried out in prior workshops. Amongst the large pieces that Garth was to rehearse on his own and present to me once somewhat formed were the lioness hunt, the hyena march, and the male hyena breakout dance for "Be Prepared," the ballet interlude for "Can You Feel the Love Tonight," the trickster dance for "I Can't Wait to be King," and the fight choreography for the grand finale. The flying sections for the ballet as well as the other flying moments in the show had to be tried out and rehearsed on a stage on 42nd Street where Foy had set up the rigging.

The dancers not only play animals, we play the grasslands, and so, in an abstract way, we are the savanna. We are not just wildebeest, we *are* the stampede. Julie has brought concert dance to the forefront of the production.

—*Aubrey Lynch,*
Dance Captain

Dancers rehearse the
highly stylized lioness hunt.

Supported by a harness, Christine Yasunaga practices flying for the aerial ballet of "Can You Feel the Love Tonight," while other dancers carry the towering fantasy giraffes for the production number "I Can't Wait to Be King."

Because Garth's choreography can be very difficult to learn and master, I would periodically check into his rehearsals to see if we were on the same wavelength. It's frustrating to have the dancers learn a piece to perfection only to have it thrown out because it's not what the director had in mind. For Garth this process was positively challenging, but also quite trying, as he is used to answering to no one but himself as the director of his own modern dance company. What was most difficult for Garth to get used to was the short amount of time alloted for many of the dance pieces. He would create these marvelous numbers that could have lived on their own in any dance concert. But in context of this book musical, some of his numbers were way too long in juxtaposition to the acting scenes that surrounded them. The rhythm of *The Lion King* script had been established in the film. The scenes were short and fast and moved along, unlike most plays. I liked this and wanted to maintain that pacing, but at the same time I wanted to give Garth enough time to create developed dances that could tell a story and exploit the tremendous talents that we had engaged. There was much trial and error for all of us to find that balance and, until we finally had the show on its feet and running in Minneapolis, we wouldn't really nail the ultimate structure and pacing.

Dancers suspended from the flies entwine romantically during "Can You Feel the Love Tonight."

The choreography for *The Lion King* is both spirited . . .

. . . and sinuous (left to right: Iresol Cardona, Camille M. Brown, Lana Gordon, Michael Joy, Ashi K. Smythe, Levensky Smith, Mark Allan Davis).

Following pages: Dancers leap exuberantly during the lioness hunt (left to right: Christine Yasunaga, Lana Gordon, Iresol Cardona, Karine Plantadit-Bageot, Endalyn Taylor-Shellman, Camille M. Brown).

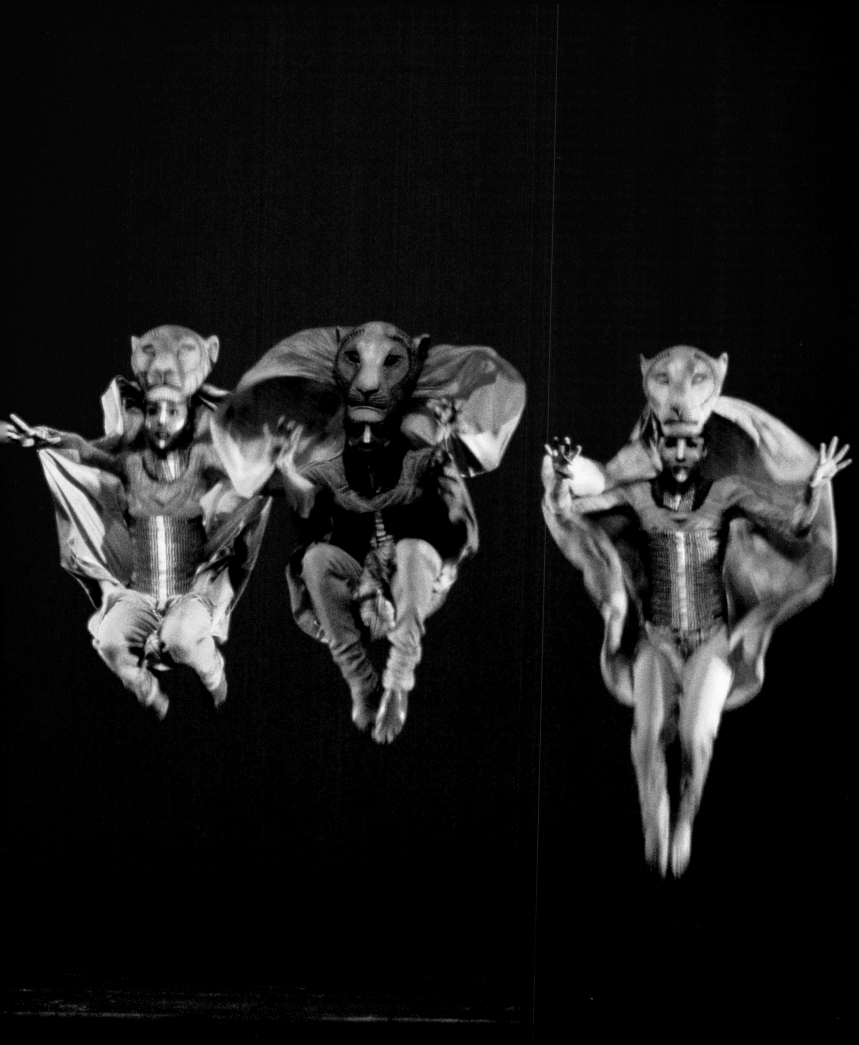

Stanley Wayne Mathis, Kevin Cahoon, and Tracy Nicole Chapman, who play the trio of hungry hyenas, rehearse with musical director Joe Church.

MUSIC REHEARSALS

For the first two weeks of rehearsals, the choral singers concentrated solely on learning their vocal parts with Lebo as choral director and arranger and Joe as overall music director. It was hard at the start for the two men to find a compatible working style. Lebo is extremely spontaneous and works out his complex harmonies and rhythms on the spot. Joe comes from a more traditional Western style of teaching and conducting and usually works from a completed score. The chorus had to learn to respond to the direction of both men and that took the usual getting used to. The individual principals would learn their music on a one-to-one basis with Joe and then they would come to me to work on integrating their songs into scenes.

Lebo's lioness and grasslands chants were created in rehearsal and, because they were linked to choreography, they were not fixed musically until all the elements came together. Usually Garth choreographs to a finished piece of music and needs the counts to be absolutely specific, so this was a bit trying at first. Ultimately, though, the back-and-forth process of music inspiring dance, and then the dance moves inspiring new twists in the music, turned out to be the best and only method in what was a truly collaborative process. Throughout the rehearsal period, Bob Elhai, one of the main orchestrators, would take down the new material and start to design the orchestrations. Mark Mancina was able to join us during the last ten days or so and helped to codify and finalize some of the musical questions.

Scott Irby-Ranniar and Sam Wright gather around Joe Church, the musical director, to run through a song.

The choral music in *The Lion King* is inspired and heavily influenced by South African culture, South African music, and South African history. The roots are very much a unique marriage of African choral styles of singing with African percussion and Eurocentric orchestrations.

In *The Lion King* film, though, the music was heavily influenced by the story itself, which was very inspiring to me as a South African (I am from Soweto). It was very much a personal story, this triumph of Simba and Mufasa. *The Lion King* project came to me at a crucial and critical time in my life and in my country's history, when serious changes were taking place. Most of the characters in the movie became human beings to me, because I associated Mufasa with Mandela, and I associated Simba with myself. I was in exile. I left home when I was 14 years old (if I hadn't left, I would have been put in jail); I went back home three years ago, an adult and a professional. It became a personal journey for me to be involved in *The Lion King*, and most of the music I wrote, and the lyrics and arrangements, are very much inspired by my life story and my background as a South African artist.

As South Africans, singing and vocalization is very much an intricate part of our lives. Much of our music was inspired many years ago by workers in the gold mines. These men went through hardships, had to live 20 to a small room in compounds, and went home only for a month each year to see their wives and children. Songs came from that era, when the South African apartheid system forced people to live in a way that dehumanized them. These people created music that was inspired by their hardships, and they inspired each other through their music. Competitions of a cappella choirs started occurring within those compounds. When I was three, four years old, my father used to take me to where the mine workers lived, because every weekend there were competitions from seven in the morning until ten at night, 200 choirs, great music and singing and dancing.

But this music in turn is based on music from very ancient times, from way before there was political oppression. Africa has various cultures and regions where various styles of music and instruments come from, and in our case, voices are our instruments.

Lebo M,
Composer

Composer Lebo M (center), Nhlanhla Ngema, and Faca Kulu perform in "One by One."

PUTTING THE PIECES TOGETHER

Once the singers and dancers had learned their music and dance choreography, they joined me in the large rehearsal room to work out their blocking and integration into the show. A number of the animal puppets for the opening "Circle of Life," such as the life-size elephant, or the twenty-foot giraffes, were too large to fit into the space, so we had to leave those scenes for Minneapolis. We also were unable to fit a full-scale mock-up of the Pride Rock set piece in the room, as well as a number of other crucial set pieces that would determine spacing. The fact that the scenery was designed to be constantly shifting meant that we had to use our imaginations in thinking through the staging and scene shifts in these first five weeks.

Even so, a number of thrilling moments came to life in that relatively small room. The first time all 27 hyenas broke into their frenzied dance, or the huge wildebeest masks were thrust high into the air by the the stomping male dancers we all felt a rush of excitement. Every day felt like Christmas as some new creature or vision came into being. As exciting as the puppets and masks were, we were all as equally impressed and moved by the spontaneity, freshness, and truth that was coming from the acting, singing, and dance moves of Scott Irby-Ranniar, our twelve-year-old Simba. It was great to watch the chorus enjoying the acting performances of the principals and the actors enjoying the

Two percussionists, Junior "Gabu" Wedderburn and Valerie Naranjo, take a break during rehearsal.

Production Stage Manager Jeff Lee presides over the script and the usual collection of coffee cups.

Top: (left) Lana Gordon as a cheetah; (center) Mark Allan Davis as a zebra; (right) leaping antelopes.

Bottom: Dancers playing tricksters and giraffes go through their paces for "I Can't Wait to Be King."

virtuosity of the dancers. Junior "Gabu" Wedderburn and Valerie Naranjo, two of our African percussionists, joined the rehearsals in the third week which brought the energy up to an even higher notch. The bonding of the company started to take shape as they began to sense the creativity and vitality at work.

By the fifth week in New York we were ready to take a stab at a run-through. With only a few assistants to help dress the company into their various head gear and puppet parts, we did manage to bring in the first run-through at under three hours. We were shocked at how smoothly it all flowed. There is a life to these first run-throughs that can never be replaced. The fact that it is all happening up close and in your face, and without the full complement of sets, lights, sound, makeup, and costumes, is a profoundly moving experience. The chorus is unamplified and will never sound better. The danger of a dancer leaping into your lap adds so much to an already highly visceral experience. Each muscle move of an actor's face is deliciously expressive and can't be seen across the orchestra pit in a 2,000-seat theater. One can only hope at this point in the process that what we were experiencing would translate onto the large stage and have the intimate, human, and emotional impact that only the rehearsal hall can give.

The producers and the artistic team observe a final run-through.

Our last day of rehearsal in New York was our second run-through, and Michael Eisner, Peter Schneider, and Tom Schumacher, as well as the writers, a few managers, and some invited guests, were in attendance. All went smoothly and after the rehearsal, the team met to discuss the status of the book, music, choreography, and performances. Varying opinions flew back and forth. Some I registered, some I dismissed, and some I felt were extremely helpful critiques that only a fresh perspective could contribute. Everyone was very enthusiastic and we all felt ready to make the next move, onto the stage of the Orpheum Theater in Minneapolis.

During a final run-through in New York, Tsidii Le Loka, playing Rafiki, calls the animals to the Circle of Life.

Following pages: Mufasa climbs the canyon walls
to escape the stampeding wildebeest.

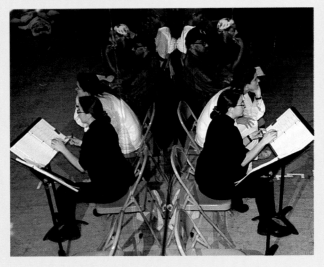

I usually work as a production stage manager, and if I don't do that I work as an assistant director. I've assisted Julie quite a few times—this is my seventh production with her—and I deal very much with the overall production, facilitating the technical aspects as well as the artistic. I facilitate communication, help problems get ironed out. Dan Fields and I really balance each other, because Dan has been with *The Lion King* from the beginning and knows as much as one can know about the show, and I know as much as one can possibly know about working with Julie.

This is a much bigger show than anything else I've worked on with Julie. It's funny to say that, because the production of the opera *Oedipus Rex* that she directed was huge: There was an 80-person chorus, and technically it was very complicated. But *The Lion King* is big in every area. The sheer number of costumes and masks is part of what makes this production so enormous.

Working with Julie is an adventure every day. She has energy like no one I have ever seen before. She can rehearse seven hours a day and work right through lunch break and then do some meetings. She never stops, and her mind never stops. After four hours at a stretch of some really difficult rehearsing and having to make decisions and answer questions about scenery, when I'm feeling completely exhausted and my brain has just shut down, I watch her and marvel that she is still going.

Watching her work in general is so exhilarating, because I find her vision to be so delightful and wonderful to watch come to life. I connect with her vision deeply. It's magical, it's very theatrical. I've heard her describe the stampede scene over and over, and when we finally started to rehearse it, well, this vision works. When you put the music and the text and the visuals of the masks and puppets finally together, it just blew me away.

She is one of the few directors I've worked with who has not only a grasp but a vast knowledge of every aspect of theater production. She has a very straightforward approach to directing—she's fairly specific about what she wants from people in terms of moving from here to there. But she's also very open. I think it's a wonderful combination of knowing what she wants overall, and yet when she goes into specific scene work, she's open to letting actors try what makes them feel comfortable. Ultimately it will be the way she wants it to be—she's not wishy-washy. In the bigger scenes, the vision is very specific and very clear, and she stages it and that's that. It's a nice combination of being open and collaborative and yet ultimately very clear about her vision.

—*Michele Steckler,*
Assistant Director

MINNEAPOLIS—THE OUT-OF-TOWN TRYOUT

By the time *The Lion King* company arrived in Minneapolis for the last three weeks of rehearsal, the scenery had been loaded into the Orpheum Theater and set up on stage, lights had been hung, and the sound system installed. Jeff Lee, our production stage manager had come a week earlier to join Richard Hudson and his team to begin what is a called a "dry tech." The idea is to move technically through the show, roughing out the scene setups and shifts, and to sketch in preliminary lighting cues. During the fifth week of rehearsals, Don Holder was flying back and forth between New York City and Minneapolis to observe our run-throughs and simultaneously focus the lights on stage. The daily reports sent to New York City from Jeff were generally positive, but there seemed to be problems with the computer functioning of the Pride Rock set piece. The last thing I was looking forward to was having to stop rehearsals for set pieces that refused to budge.

On June 14, my assistant directors and I traveled to Minneapolis, the actors to follow the next day. We spent the afternoon meeting the crew, inspecting and walking the set, and reviewing some of the major cues. It's always an overwhelming experience to see the set for the first time. Through what is probably intense trepidation and fear of everything that can go wrong, it's not unnatural to have an instant love/hate relationship with your new challenge. With my total enthusiasm, Richard had designed a set of infinite options as to the look, and Don had a blank cyc (a blank canvas) and six surrounding light boxes that also offered myriad choices as to the color of the lighting. We now had three weeks to develop and complete the total picture.

That night, in reaction to something I ate, not the impending technical rehearsal, I had intense stomach and chest pains which turned out to be a nasty gallstone that had to be removed, along with my gallbladder. The operation was the next day: the first day of tech.

The Orpheum Theater in Minneapolis, where *The Lion King* company performs the show for the first time.

After surgery: discussions with
Thomas Schumacher aboard a special recliner.
Below: Backstage at the Orpheum, an
imaginative storage system has elephants and
gazelles dangling high above the wings.

TECHNICAL REHEARSALS

As the computer system for the set still needed some software fine-tuning, the actors spent the first day of tech in a rehearsal hall down the street while I remained in bed. By day three we were all ready to begin, even though the set and I still weren't completely up to snuff. The producers had rented me a giant black leather reclining chair that they promptly set up in the middle of the auditorium. This picture set a somewhat sympathetic and comic tone for the start of tech. From my reclining position, microphone at my mouth, I began the process of moving everyone through the show, moment by moment. Decisions had to be made on each light cue, each entrance wing for an actor, the speed of a drop that flies in from above, or of an elevator that rises out of the deck, the position of a scenic piece and the timing for its disappearance, the paint job on the deck and on the walls of Pride Rock, among other things.

With a host of computers sitting on large boards spread out over the seats, and headsets to communicate backstage, we were able to begin tracking the cues. While I, the designers, the production stage manager, and choreographer operate from the auditorium, the crew, stage managers, and performers are getting used to the idiosyncracies of the stage deck, the mountains and traps they have to ascend and descend, and the limited backstage space they have to conquer for the numerous costume changes that occur. Wardrobe stations in the wings and under the stage are designated as there will not be enough time for the actors to get to their dressing rooms for the quick changes.

During tech rehearsals, Michael Ward works with the actors in the makeup room, doing tests and teaching them how to apply their own elaborate makeup. Mary, Tracy, and the wardrobe staff led by Kjeld Anderson continue to have fittings, make alterations, and organize the tracking sheets for the eighteen dressers who will work backstage during the show. Michael Curry and the carpenters figure out the elaborate storage system for the puppets in the wings that, when finished, looks like either the most wonderful flying zoo, or a bizarre slaughterhouse with gazelles hung upside down on suspended racks.

Tech time, especially on my shows, can prove quite frustrating for the actors because the pace is tedious, the attention is to the technical matters and not the acting, and the hours are long—up to twelve hours a day. Actually for the crew and the artistic team, especially the lighting designer, the day starts at 8:00 A.M.

and ends at midnight. Each scene has some obstacle to overcome. Among our crises were:

- The elephant is too big to enter the door into the auditorium. A stage manager will have to guide it in as the actors inside the legs bow down and walk single file down the narrow aisle. Still works as a great image for the top of the show.
- The actress playing Sarabi is afraid of heights. She has to ascend Pride Rock with Mufasa. It is fifteen feet high with no railings and it moves. Give her time, she will overcome it. She did.
- The shadow puppet of little Simba that is supposed to appear in the tree looks terrible, is hard to light, and we couldn't hide the puppeteer. Solution? Cut it. Richard Hudson paints the image on a piece of muslin. We backlight it. Simpler. Elegant. And why didn't we just do that in the first place?
- The ground rows, which looked so great in the model, eat up too much space off stage. Cut them. Richard designs smaller ones. All is not lost.

(A quick note about the art of cutting scenic items. I'm not big on it. It's too expensive. I believe that with good planning you can avoid the shocking truth that things might not work. On the other hand you can't always know every-thing in advance and one needs to take risks and try for the best. But if your best isn't working, cut it. Fast).

- The two kids are supposed to fly during the production number for "I Can't Wait to Be King." Scott keeps getting snagged on the tree branch in the wings and both kids keep spinning around in circles because of the type of flying rig and the limited flying space above. The timing of the

Above: During technical rehearsals in Minneapolis, Scott Irby-Ranniar and Kajuana Shuford practice riding on the spectacularly tall giraffes, while Geoff Hoyle and the Zazu puppet (lower left) watch from positions of relative safety.

Left: The largest elephant—measuring 13 feet long, 11 feet 3 inches high, and 9 feet wide at the ears—parades down the aisle of the theater.

In the Orpheum's dressing rooms, Scott Irby-Ranniar and Kajuana Shuford receive attention from makeup artists.

music is too fast for Scott to fly down and snatch the bird puppet out of Zazu's hands. The harnesses are pinching the less than meaty bodies of our two young actors. Is it all worth it? Do we have enough time to perfect it? Can we ever overcome the lack of control that the two young actors will have over their movements? No. No. And no. Cut the flying in this scene. Scott will stay on the floor, Kujuana, young Nala, will remain on the back of the ostrich. Scott's a great dancer and now the scene can really focus around him. A very good cut. Except that that means the giant suspended giraffes have to go, too. We'll put them in the lobby of the New Amsterdam, when we go to New York.

- The giant moving bone staircase in the elephant graveyard is killing the backs of our dancers who have to move it during the hyena chase scene. Too heavy. Bad casters. Bumps in the deck that can't be avoided. Solution? Put it on a central pivot point so that the dancers don't have to work so hard and there is no danger of it crashing into the side lightboxes.

- Biggest problem in Act One: The scene and costume change from the end of the hyena bacchanal in "Be Prepared" to the start of the stampede of the wildebeests. We always knew that this was going to be tough. Based on the given estimate of three minutes, I had designed a nonverbal transition scene that could happen downstage in front of a full-stage shadow screen. That means that the crew would have the whole upstage to set up the canyon and the wildebeest rollers. It's not that the giraffe shadow puppets and the downstage walkby of the cheetah and full-scale giraffe weren't winning. They were fine, but for two or three minutes at most. Even after a few go rounds this scene and mega-costume change was coming in at ten minutes. Phone call to Roger and Irene. We need a new scene to cover the transition. Solution for the first week of previews: a scheduled pause, as in opera. After that a new scene was created for Mufasa and Zazu which, surprisingly, did not turn out to be just filler but, instead, a rather comical and moving scene that adds to the development of these characters.

- The bug boxes: Somehow these whimsical jack-in-the-boxes that were supposed to glide in on a track and pop open at Timon's instigation to reveal grubs and other insect delectibles during "Hakuna Matata" turned out to be the white elephant of prop design. Hard to put the blame on any one person, but not only were these bug boxes incredibly ugly, they didn't work. And they had cost a lot. We had them remade in Minneapolis. Still ugly and still no popping. A makeshift solution was created for the run in Minneapolis and we await new, beautiful bug boxes for New York. (The bug boxes stood out as one of the only prop or puppet designs that had somehow slipped through the cracks in what is a show with hundreds of complicated and sophisticated inventions. I only bring it up as an example of annoyance because, in fact, this type of failure was so rare.)

The hyenas give their allegiance to Scar (John Vickery) during the song "Be Prepared." Following pages: Scar (John Vickery) surveys his skeleton-ridden domain.

Coordinating action and lights during the waterfall sequence proved to be a technical challenge.

- The waterfall: a scene that could never be rehearsed in New York, it was probably the most complicated bit of action with the least amount of stage time. Suffice it to say that every part of this scene, from the appearance of a rushing river that sweeps the live Timon offstage to the appearance of the miniature Timon puppet dangling from a branch over a vibrating silk waterfall that drops down to a pool of snapping crocodiles, to the transformation of the waterfall via projections and light alteration to the flashback of the stampede and Mufasa's death . . . suffice it to say that this bit of important new psychological storytelling became one of the most difficult action scenes to structure and operate and perform. Once we were able to work out all the various complicated riggings, the meticulous timing of each event was critical. If the timing was off, for even two seconds, the entire impact of the scene would not work. More startling were audiences that occasionally interrupted the flow of events by applauding at the sight of the waterfall. It's very hard at that point to lead them to the seriousness of the scene when they are enrapt by the scenery. Previews allowed us to get the rhythm down right.

- The climactic battle scene between Scar and Simba was rehearsed in New York City to take place on the moving elephant staircase. Of course we hadn't rehearsed it on the actual scenic piece so our plan existed in theory only. Once confronted with the difficulty of moving this huge staircase around, let alone restoring it in the wings after the battle, we quickly saw that another solution needed to be found. While watching the giant shadow screen move about the stage, the idea of having the two characters perform their final confrontation on the top edge of the screen kept taunting us. It made artistic sense; the shadow screen, which suggests Pride Rock in an abstract way, would actually become the mountain off of which Scar falls. But it seemed like an impossible feat. The two actors would both have to be harnessed and the screen would have to be exactly in line with the track of the fly lines. Not impossible. But the screen is a stretched piece of fabric. The actors would need to have another hard structure, a metal frame that would be moved into position behind the shadow screen upon which they could solidly place their feet and keep their balance. Once the frame was made our two actors were game. It was a nightmare to rehearse but the danger of the scene is exciting and serves the script well.

Every night, after a long day of tech, the artistic and stage managerial team would get together to assess how far we had progressed, what the problems were, and what would be the next day's plan of attack. As tech had been delayed a few days it seemed as if we would never make the appointed dress rehearsals, which would be our only rehearsals with full orchestra before the first preview. At these moments there is always pressure to move faster and to take less time with each light cue. The myth that everything can be fixed in previews raises its deceptive head and the tension rises. The fact is, at least in

Donald Holder's lighting suffuses stomping hyenas with a hellish glow.

Skeletal gazelles catch the light and form a stark silhouette against the African horizon. Christine Yasunaga pushes the gazelle wheel.

my experience and in my style of theater, that without getting overly fussy, it is absolutely essential that you not skip over cues that you know have to be there because, in reality, you never get back there again. Preview rehearsals should be for fine tuning the light cues and, more important, should be time for the focus to return to the performers. Given the complications and ambitions of the piece, Don, Jeff, and I felt that we were moving as fast as we could. Even though I had no serious doubts that we would be ready, it did seem miraculous when we finally arrived at our first dress rehearsal.

Drought in the pridelands:
Mark Allan Davis bears a buzzard pole
as a pool of water, made of silk,
disappears into a hole in the stage.

PREVIEWS

Two days later our first audience had taken their seats in high anticipation. By this time our whole crew, including producers and performers, were a little frazzled, exhausted, and not quite sure how it all would play. We'd become inured to the beautiful pictures, the delicate nuances of performances, and the lowbrow jokes. Anything could happen with the functioning of the computer which operated the set; it seemed to have a mind if its own. So, with headset on, Michele sits on my left, notepad in hand, ready to take the technical notes.

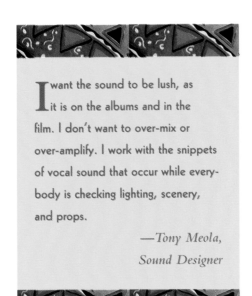

And Dan sits on my right, ready to take the sound and actor notes. Butterflies.

The curtain rises and Rafiki starts her chant. From the balcony Lebo and Faca, under their antelope headdresses, chant back. Clouds float upward one at a time to reveal the sun rising. Two giraffes emerge and slowly move across the stage, silhouetted by the large golden globe. The audience starts to clap and cheer. The large elephant lumbers down the aisle followed by the wildebeests and bird ladies. Heads are turning madly all around us. More applause. And again for the gazelles that leap across the stage. Another wave of applause from the balcony as they finally are able to see the elephant as he climbs up onto the deck. Rafiki starts to sing the familiar refrain of "Circle of Life" and they cheer again. We can hardly hear the song through the racket of the audience. It is overwhelming after two years of work and anticipation. I turn to Dan and Michele. We are stunned.

There were plenty of technical notes that night but we knew that the basic performance was there. Our goal over the next three weeks of previews was to make certain cuts in some of the dance numbers, to work on the balance of sound, to reorchestrate some of the songs in order to achieve the desired climax, to fiddle with dialogue, and to rehearse the new scene that would eventually replace the pause in Act One. There were also technical glitches during those early performances that needed to be worked out. A few examples of these stomach-churning events:

- The mountain wouldn't rise (due to computer malfunction) causing Pride Rock to look like a mole hill that night.
- Mufasa had to climb the canyon wall using his own strength because the fly lines which support him had gotten tangled.
- The cactuses wouldn't inflate on cue.
- The king curtain, which is supposed to drop from the flies, got caught halfway and a stagehand, unbeknownst to the audience, had to climb out onto the grid during the show to untangle it.

And so on. These are the normal crises that eventually work themselves out. But the hardest challenge for everyone was the flow backstage. For a week or so, I declined the invitation to watch the chaos from the wings. I suspected that if I was confronted with all the misery up close it would be hard to keep pushing everyone to achieve the desired quick costume changes or complicated set changes. I knew that eventually they would get the rhythm down.

When the dust seemed settled and the look of confusion and despair had disappeared from the dressers' faces, I ventured backstage to see the "other show." In an odd way I was more moved by that experience than in watching the musical from the house. It was so utterly real. So dangerous. An intensely beautiful ballet of human and mechanical interaction without an inch of space unoccupied. While the children sang their "I Just Can't Wait to Be King" song downstage, in front of the black drop, the stagehands, in time to the music, would be setting up the huge bones of the elephant graveyard. The absurd juxtaposition was startling but the incongruity had created another performance all of its own. From the audience's perspective, a perfect illusion was being performed, but from backstage the reality of making that illusion work was palpably raw, happening-in-the-moment, fundamentally live theater.

At the conclusion of the performance, I felt I had to go to the intercom to tell the company, both crew and performers, how moved I was by how they had surmounted the mechanics of running such an extremely difficult show. I'm sure I got quite maudlin over that intercom as I thanked them for helping to bring all of our visions to fruition, but that night was one of the most profoundly moving theater experiences I have ever had.

OPENING NIGHT

We were ready to open. That's a rare statement for me. This was the first time I truly felt that, even if every little detail wasn't perfect, the company, the crew, and myself had rehearsed enough. Under our belts were a month of preview performances and endless hours of rehearsals. There is a point where the exhaustion starts to set in and it can be dangerous to the health of the performers. We had experienced the trauma and excitement of understudies suddenly having to go on for injured dancers. Spirits remained high. Costumes were finally finished, makeup designs finalized, and the set was behaving well. The show was running smoothly and we could all breathe a little bit easier.

July 31, 1997. Minneapolis. Opening night.

Glorious.

Following pages: Young Simba (Scott Irby-Ranniar) and young Nala (Kajuana Shuford) ride prancing ostriches during "I Can't Wait to Be King," while a confused Zazu (Geoff Hoyle) protests.

OFF TO BROADWAY

At the end of August we will close the show in Minneapolis and set our sights to the New Amsterdam Theater on 42nd Street. The cast is champing at the bit to go home and looking forward to the three-week hiatus while the set is being loaded into the theater. There's a big production meeting to finalize the changes in the set, script, music, and choreography. I don't believe there will be many changes but there are definite ideas that need to wait for New York to be re-rehearsed. The first order of business on the regathering of the troupe will be the cast album. Then we'll have a few days in the rehearsal rooms to review and make any acting and dancing alterations. Then back into tech with a whole new backstage crew. And this time the backstage is even smaller. Much smaller. A number of adjustments will have to be made, and the crew and cast will get to know each other really well.

As I come to the end of this often technical account of the making of *The Lion King* I want to add a few words about the company. In a collaboration as immense as this one, it is rare to have a unity that sizzles with such support, enthusiasm, and spirit. As hard as the work was, and will continue to be, it has been one of the most thoroughly gratifying experiences for all of us. The South African contingent of our performing cast, led by Lebo M, has made our piece an international, cross-cultural collaboration. Through their passion, talent, and unique artisitic contributions, they have brought the work to another level that has widened all of our horizons.

From my direction of Shakespeare plays to international opera productions in multiple languages, to my five years in Indonesia and the Far East, I have spent my theatrical life devoted to theater that crosses age, race, class, and cultural boundaries. *The Lion King*, as a story, is archetypal, and as a production includes techniques and inspirations drawn from the world theater. It aspires to speak to the experience of anyone, any family, or any tribe.

After the hard work, a time for celebration. July 4th.

Opposite page: A flock of birds proudly at rest in front of the glorious circle of the sun (Michael Joy).

SAM WRIGHT: MUFASA (opposite page, top)

Instead of trying to project something into the mask, it just became
a part of everything I did. Julie is very good at allowing you to find
the right movements, and one day I just forgot the mask was there.

JOHN VICKERY: SCAR (right)

You do what you normally do as an actor—try to figure out
motivations and character—then sing, and then add the mask movement.
But as a performer, it's fun to play with those presentational things.

HEATHER HEADLEY AND JASON RAIZE
(opposite page, bottom)

HEATHER: I find Nala really strong. From the time
she was young, she knew one day she would be a queen.
She isn't scared of anyone, she's the one who stands up to Scar.

JASON: One of the first things I thought about was that it would
be hard to transfer a lot of the scenes in the film to the stage.
In the film, when Simba and Nala meet again as adults, they have
a wild fight scene. But Garth walked in and choreographed an amazing
fight scene, which is extremely physical, but touching at the end.

HEATHER: And, of course, Nala wins the fight.

Kajuana Shuford (left) as Young Nala and Scott Irby-Ranniar as Young Simba.

Gina Breedlove as Sarabi.

TSIDII LE LOKA: RAFIKI

Rafiki is a healer, but not only in the sense of being a doctor. She is the healer spiritually, she is a guide. She is also the person who sees beyond the now in terms of time and the broad spectrum of things. Rafiki not only possesses the wisdom and maturity of a human being who is much older, but she also encompasses enough youthful energy to connect all kinds of people.

As a South African, as a person whose history is very connected to this story, it gives me a dimension to bring to the role. But as a person who has been in America for six years, who has lived in the culture and felt at home, who has been growing and learning and absorbing, that is also not insignificant to this part.

So even if I am drawing from cultural elements that give the role of Rafiki a certain edge, I am also drawing from my understanding of being a child of this American culture, even for a brief time. I believe that every culture finds a central figure who brings us to that common experience which we want to impart to our children and pass on into society.

GEOFF HOYLE: ZAZU

Zazu is the last vestige of colonialism on the African continent. The role involves doing so many things at the same time: singing, acting, dancing, and puppetry. When it all falls into place, the puppet takes on a life of its own, and it's a magical moment.

TOM ROBBINS: PUMBAA

Pumbaa is the essence of Hakuna Matata-ness. The mechanics of this puppet are so well designed, even for someone like me who has never worked with puppets before. I got the hang of it; I sort of just let go and acted.

MAX CASELLA: TIMON

Timon is like a vaudeville character in the jungle. At first, it was hard working with puppets, and the first week was kind of hellish in terms of being frustrated and confused.

And then it started to click. It's been an interesting exercise in projecting my emotion and body movements into this foreign body. I don't mind so much anymore that they're not looking at me, they're looking at my puppet. Because now I've made the puppet part of me.

Left to right: Kevin Cahoon as Ed, Tracy Nicole Chapman as Shenzi, Stanley Wayne Mathis as Banzai.

Lush jungle foliage performed by (this page, top) Ntomb'khona Dlamini, (bottom) Vanessa Jones, (opposite page, clockwise from upper left) Camille M. Brown, Lana Gordon, Iresol Cardona, Sam McKelton, Lindiwe Dlamini.

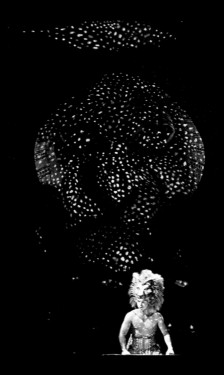

A F T E R W O R D

Six P.M., October 15. In two hours we will have our first New York preview. A few last words to round up the *Lion King* saga:

It is rare to have an opportunity to experiment, take risks, and develop a piece of theatrical art that is intended to be commercial as well. The merging of these two worlds is a rare phenomenon. Only with the enthusiastic and involved support of producers Thomas Schumacher and Peter Schneider, and with the blessing of Michael Eisner, were we, the creative team, able to realize our ideas.

I thank them for believing in my vision and backing it wholeheartedly.

Julie Taymor

Disney
PRESENTS

THE LION KING

Music & Lyrics by
ELTON JOHN & TIM RICE

Additional Music & Lyrics by
LEBO M, MARK MANCINA, JAY RIFKIN, JULIE TAYMOR, HANS ZIMMER

Book by
ROGER ALLERS & IRENE MECCHI

Starring

JOHN VICKERY   SAMUEL E. WRIGHT

GEOFF HOYLE   TSIDII LE LOKA   TOM ALAN ROBBINS

JASON RAIZE   HEATHER HEADLEY

STANLEY WAYNE MATHIS   TRACY NICOLE CHAPMAN   KEVIN CAHOON

SCOTT IRBY-RANNIAR   KAJUANA SHUFORD

and

MAX CASELLA

KEVIN BAILEY   EUGENE BARRY-HILL   GINA BREEDLOVE   CAMILLE M. BROWN   IRESOL CARDONA
ALBERTO CRUZ, Jr.   MARK ALLAN DAVIS   LINDIWE DLAMINI   NTOMB'KHONA DLAMINI   SHEILA GIBBS
LANA GORDON   LINDIWE HLENGWA   TIMOTHY HUNTER   CHRISTOPHER JACKSON   JENNIFER JOSEPHS
VANESSA A. JONES   MICHAEL JOY   FACA KULU   RON KUNENE   SONYA LESLIE   AUBREY LYNCH II
PHILIP DORIAN McADOO   SAM McKELTON   PETER ANTHONY MOORE   NANDI MORAKE   NHLANHLA NGEMA
KARINE PLANTADIT-BAGEOT   DANNY RUTIGLIANO   LEVENSKY SMITH   ASHI K. SMYTHE
ENDALYN TAYLOR-SHELLMAN   RACHEL TECORA TUCKER   FRANK WRIGHT II   CHRISTINE YASUNAGA   and LEBO M

Adapted from the screenplay by
IRENE MECCHI & JONATHAN ROBERTS & LINDA WOOLVERTON

Scenic Design	*Costume Design*	*Lighting Design*	*Mask & Puppet Design*
RICHARD HUDSON	JULIE TAYMOR	DONALD HOLDER	JULIE TAYMOR & MICHAEL CURRY

Sound Design	*Hair & Makeup Design*	*Casting*
TONY MEOLA	MICHAEL WARD	JAY BINDER

Technical Director	*Production Stage Manager*	*Press Representative*
DAVID BENKEN	JEFF LEE	BONEAU/BRYAN-BROWN

Music Director	*Orchestrators*	*Music Coordinator*
JOSEPH CHURCH	ROBERT ELHAI DAVID METZGER BRUCE FOWLER	MICHAEL KELLER

Music Produced for the Stage & Additional Score by
MARK MANCINA

Associate Music Producer
ROBERT ELHAI

Additional Vocal Score, Vocal Arrangements & Choral Director
LEBO M

Choreography by
GARTH FAGAN

Directed by
JULIE TAYMOR

WALT DISNEY THEATRICAL PRODUCTIONS

President	Peter Schneider
Executive Vice President	Thomas Schumacher
Creative Affairs	Stuart Oken
General Manager	Alan Levey
Production Supervisors	Bob Routolo, John Tiggeloven
Business Affairs	Kevin Breen, Gabrielle Klatsky, Harry Gold, Robbin Kelley, Dan Posener, Karen Lewis
Labor Relations	John Petrafesa, Sr., Robert W. Johnson, Leslie Ann Bennett
Marketing	Ron Kollen, Deb Axtell, Frank Conway, Jack Eldon, Kim First
International	Skip Malone, Andrew Fell, Martyn Hayes
Finance	Clark Spencer, Amy Copeland, Shimanti Guha, David Schrader, Alan Guno, Steven Klein, Scott Savoie, Ron Villarreal
Development	Alice Jankell, Michelle Mindlin, Michael Sanfilippo
Group Sales	Chip Brown, Leslie Case, Tami Carlson
Administrative Staff	Elliot Altman, Jane T.N. Collins, Stephanie Cheek, Carl Flanigan, Priscilla Garriga, Jay Hollenback, Debbie Hoy, Stacie Iverson, Connie Jasper, Risa Kelly, Aaron Levin, Diane Mellen, Patti Mills, Mary Ann Parsons, Mary Lou Pawley, Danielle Pinnt, Roberta Risafi, Robyn Ruehl, Andy Temesvary, Susan Tyker, Marianne Virtuoso, Derek Wadlington, Pam Waterman, Julianna Wineland

STAFF FOR THE LION KING

Associate Producer	Donald B. Frantz
Project Manager	Nina Essman

GENERAL PRESS REPRESENTATIVES
BONEAU/BRYAN-BROWN
Chris Boneau • Patty Onagan • Jackie Green
Miguel Tuason • Joel Hile

Company Manager	STEVEN CHAIKELSON
Assistant Company Manager	Johanna Pfaelzer
Stage Manager	Mahlon Kruse
Stage Manager	Elizabeth Burgess
Stage Manager	Steve 'Doc' Zorthian
Assistant Directors	Dan Fields, Michele Steckler
Assistant Choreographer	Norwood J. Pennewell, Natalie Rogers
Dance Captain	Aubrey Lynch II
Assistant Dance Captain	Rachel Tecora Tucker
Management Associate	Nick Lobel-Weiss
Associate Scenic Designers	Peter Eastman, Jonathan Fensom
Scenic Design Assistants	Catherine Chung, David Cozier, Sarah Eckert, Michael Fagin, Paul Kelly, Hyun-Joo-Kim, Mark Nayden, Steve Olson, Atkin Pace, Russell Parkman, Dawn Petrlik
Associate Lighting Designer	Jeanne Koenig Rubin
Assistant Lighting Designer	Martin Vreeland
Lighting Design Assistant	Karen Spahn
Projection Designer	Geoff Puckett
Projection Art	Caterina Bertolotto
Assistant Sound Designer	Kai Harada
Associate Costume Designer	Mary Nemecek Peterson
Assistant Costume Designer	Tracy Dorman
Costume Design Assistants	Kristian Kraai, Marion Williams
Mask/Puppet Studio Dept. Heads	Pete Beeman, Loren Bevans, Sue Bonde, Jeff Curry, Liza Pastine, Mark Spivey, Debra Tennenbaum
Mask/Puppet Craftspeople	Emily Bank, Roi Bobiak, Debra Bruneaux, Katia Debear, Gary Graham, Debrah Glassberg, Patricia Gropusso, Paul Jenkins, Brett Kahler, Steven Kaplan, Maria Klein, Gabriel Koren, Sky Lanigan, David Laubenthal, Nelson Lowry, Mike Marsh, Brad Pace, Anne Salt, Manju Shandler, Cyndee Starr, Mari Tobita, Christopher Webb
Design Studio Coordinator	Jason Scott Eagan

Associate Technical Director	Stephen M. Detmer
Production Carpenter	Drew Siccardi
Automation	Rick Howard
Assistant Carpenters	Steven McEntee, Michael Trotto
Automation Carpenters	Steven Stackle, George Zegarsky
Production Flyman	Brad Ingram
Production Electrician	James Maloney
Key Spot Operator	Joseph P. Garvey
Board Operator	Edward M. Greenberg
Automated Lighting Technician	Sean Strohmeyer
Automated Lighting Programmer	Aland Henderson
Automated Lighting Tracker	Lara Bohon
Production Propman	Victor Amerling
Assistant Propman	Baron Becker
Production Sound Engineer	Scott Stauffer
Assistant Sound Engineer	Marie Renée Foucher
Wardrobe Supervisor	Kjeld Andersen
Assistant Wardrobe Supervisor/ Puppet Master	Louis Troisi
Hair Supervisor	John "Jack" Curtin
Assistant Hair Supervisor	Monte C. Haught
Makeup Supervisor	Kate Chittenden
Assistant Makeup Supervisor	Elizabeth Cohen
Production Assistants	Ryan Baker, Genoveva Castañeda, Carrie Christensen, Theresa Gonzales, Hillary Knill, Lisa Koch, Gabriel Koren, Benjamin Krevolin, Bev Jensen, Annie McKilligan, Babette Roberts, Elizabeth Rohr, Ria Tyriver, Susan Vargo, Justin Wilkes
Production Interns	Bill Augustin, Ilyse Bosch, Bo Yin Chan, Carly Dranginis, Michael Duffy, Christopher Economakos, James Festante, Ari Glazer, Kimberly Gordon, Nicole Hudson, Vinny Iaropoli, Sara Kannenberg, Wayne Knaub, Matthew Legreca, Maiko Matsushima, Felicia Pearce, Melissa Ring, Andrea Sarubbi, Mark E. Smith, Jennifer Tonnensen, Janine Vanderhoff, Jacob Williams, Christina Wong
SSDC Observers	Caden Manson, Melanie Martin
Executive Music Producer	Chris Montan
Music Development	Nick Glennie-Smith
Music Preparation	Donald Oliver & Evan Morris Chelsea Music Service, Inc.
Synthesizer Programmer	Ted Baker
Orchestral Synthesizer Programmer	Christopher Ward
Electronic Drum Programmer	Tommy Igoe
Additional Percussion Arrangements	Valerie Dee Naranjo
Music Assistant	Elizabeth J. Falcone
Personal Assistant to Elton John	Bob Halley
Assistant to Tim Rice	Eileen Heinink
Assistant to Mark Mancina	Robbie Boyd
Associate Casting Director	Mark Brandon
Casting Associates	Jack Bowden, Amy Kitts
Casting Assistant	Laura Stanczyk
Stunt Consultant	Peter Moore
Physical Therapy	Sean Gallagher—Performing Arts Physical Therapy, Inc.
Orthopedist	Dr. Philip Bauman
Assistant to Associate Producer	Alice A. Farrell
Corporate Counsel	Michael Rosenfeld
Production Accountants	Dolores Salkow, Ann Caprio
Banking	Barbara Von Borstel, Morgan Guaranty Trust Co.
Children's Tutoring	On Location Education
Child Guardian	Dale Kimber
Press Assistants	Patrick Paris, Alison McDonald
Production Photography	Joan Marcus, Marc Bryan-Brown
Documentary Photography/Video	Kenneth Van Sickle
Merchandising	Disney Consumer Products

Copyright © 1997 Disney Enterprises, Inc.

All rights reserved. No part of this book may be used or
reproduced in any manner whatsoever without the written
permission of the Publisher. For information address:
Disney Editions
114 Fifth Avenue
New York, New York 10011

FOR HYPERION:

Editor: WENDY LEFKON
Assistant Editor: ROBIN FRIEDMAN
Director of Preproduction: LESLEY KRAUSS
Design Manager: CLAUDYNE BEDELL
Production Editor: DAVID LOTT
Director of Production: LINDA PRATHER

Photo Editing and Book Design: BTD/BETH TONDREAU

ISBN 0-7868-6342-0

First Edition

10   9   8   7   6

DRAWINGS AND RENDERINGS BY JULIE TAYMOR:

pp. 31–38, 54, 55, 57–61, 68, 69, 71, 72, 82–83, 87–93, 123

PHOTO CREDITS:

PER BREIEHAGEN—pp. 17, 57 (Gina Breedlove),
58 (Jason Raize as Simba), 59 (Heather Headley),
70 (Stanley Wayne Mathis), 184, 185, 186, 187, 188, 189

STEVE LABUZETTA—p. 49 (Garth Fagan)

JOAN MARCUS—pp. 1, 2–3, 4–5, 6–7, 8–9, 10–11, 12, 16,
62–63, 70 (close-up of mask), 75, 84–85, 94–95, 102, 110–111,
115, 135 (grasslands), 141, 143, 144 (Simba and Scar), 145,
146–147, 151, 152, 153, 154–155, 157, 162–163, 169, 170–171,
173, 178–179, 181, 182–183, 190, 191

All others: KENNETH VAN SICKLE

Pages 18–19: Fabric hand-painted by
J. MICHELLE HILL-CAMPBELL

Pages 46–47: Fabric for red giraffes hand-painted by
WARREN JORGENSON

Pages 128–129: Fabric dyed by
JOAN MORRIS